CHAPTER ONE

"Well, then... I *suppose* you should try them on."
Dad looks blankly at the *best shoes in the world*.

OK. *This* bit has gone surprisingly well, which
makes me nervous. I did actually *need* new school
shoes (and it has nothing to do with Olivia Jones
saying my old ones came from the pound shop).
She's such an *idiot* – they don't even *sell* shoes in
our local pound shop, so the joke's on her.

But anyway, it's still really unlike Dad to suddenly
take me out to the shops on a Saturday afternoon.
But here we are: *I've got him into a shoe shop*. The
downside is he's being his typical stickler self about
it.

"I think it's definitely these ones, Dad." I try
to sound cheerful yet nonchalant. "They're so

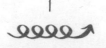

practical," I add, inspired. (Sometimes it helps to use the words they like, and my dad *really* likes things that are practical.)

I am SO close to getting the shoes. I can *taste* it. Well, not taste it, that would be gross. But you know what I mean.

Dad looks at my feet and a flicker of confusion crosses his face. "Are you sure these are regulation school uniform?"

"Yes. *Definitely*," I reply. *Come on, Dad*, I will silently. *I'm THIRTEEN. It's time for me to have cool shoes.*

OK, I don't know what the shoe craze is at your school, but at mine it's these shoes called *Jay-Shees*. They're like a plain flat shoe but sort of with a twist. The way the sole is done makes them look ever so slightly like a platform (which is *perfect* for me because I can't walk in heels). Then they have this tiny little red label sort of sticking out at the side near the back, so that everyone knows you're wearing *Jay-Shees*.

"I think I'd better just check this list again." Dad whips out his new smartphone that *I helped him set up*. "No, it says here the shoes must be black and

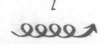

WHEN GOOD GEEKS GO BAD

CATHERINE WILKINS

nosy
crow

For Phoebe and Ernie. C.W.

First published in the UK in 2019 by Nosy Crow Ltd
The Crow's Nest, 14 Baden Place, Crosby Row,
London SE1 1YW, UK

Nosy Crow and associated logos are trademarks and/or registered
trademarks of Nosy Crow Ltd

Text © Catherine Wilkins, 2019
Cover illustration © Joel Holland, 2019

1 3 5 7 9 10 8 6 4 2

A CIP catalogue record for this book is available from the British Library

Printed and bound in Great Britain by Clays Ltd, Elcograf S.p.A.
Typeset by Tiger Media

Papers used by Nosy Crow are made from wood grown in
sustainable forests.

ISBN: 978 1 78800 059 8

www.nosycrow.com

have no other colours on them at all."

What kind of MONSTER keeps an email of a "school uniform reminder" for six months filed neatly in a folder marked with his daughter's name?! This is frankly no way to repay my kindness.

"They're fine," I assert, trying not to sound cross.

"I'm concerned about this red bit." Dad points towards the cool label. "I don't want you to get in trouble."

"That's the *best* bit. Look, *everyone* has these, Dad, even *Jas* has these. And they never get told off about it. I'm more likely to get in trouble for *not* having them." (This is true, but not with the teachers.)

"No, I don't think so," he says. "It's too much of a risk. Let's just get the plain Clarks shoes." He nods at the hovering shoe assistant.

So *this* is what I get for helping old people with modern technology.

∞∞∞↘

"I hate them, Jas," I say again, as we walk to the swimming pool on Sunday morning.

Quite often on Sunday mornings Jas and I go swimming. It takes half an hour to walk there, but we worked out that if we walk it, we can spend our bus fare on crisps. (Plus it suits my dad, because that's when he does all the washing.)

She gently mocks me. "So you're wearing them because…?"

"To break them in of course," I assert. My dad has always been very clear on the perils of not breaking in shoes. This is why I always carry plasters, just in case.

"Ha. Geek," teases Jas, amused.

"Oh, Jaaaaas," I whimper-moan. "I really hate them."

"I *know*." Jas is starting to sound like I might have reached the end of her patience now. "I can tell from how you keep saying it, and from all the texts you kept sending me yesterday."

I did send Jas quite a lot of emojis of fire and angry faces yesterday. And even though Jas thinks I overreacted to Olivia's pound-shop comment, she did still send me back a lady's shoe, loads of crying faces and some hearts. We're such close best friends that sometimes we can communicate *without* words. (Though every now and then I get confused by emojis and do need the words again. Don't tell anyone in my generation I said that.)

"Like, I know it sucks," says Jas carefully. "But also, it's not the end of the world."

"I know," I concede glumly.

But also, part of me thinks unfairly and crossly, that's easy for *her* to say – she already *has* cool shoes.

My best friend Jasmine has the nicest family in the world. They're basically like the Indian Waltons. I'm assuming. I've never actually watched *The Waltons*. But I gather they're meant to be a really wholesome, kind family, who love each other.

My parents are about to get divorced and my mum has totally abandoned me. I mean, OK, so she is just living in a flat on the other side of town (because Dad lives nearer my school, and stability and continuity *blah blah blah*, and Mum's finding herself, or her feet, while she starts a new business or *whatever*). But the upshot is she's *disappeared* and I just don't seem to fit her new lifestyle. I haven't seen her for months.

Anyway. Look, I'm not getting into it now. I'm going *swimming*.

So even though the Chandrasekhars are kind of strict in some ways and expect Jas and her brothers to get good grades, they're also really generous and totally fine with them owning fun stuff. Which seems to me like a pretty good deal.

My dad expects me to get good grades with no money, treats or cool stuff incentivising me *whatsoever*. (Unless you count the occasional chocolate milkshake at Betty-Anne's Tea Shop.) And while I am very pro chocolate milkshakes, it's just, I'm thirteen now and my dad really should up his game.

The trouble is, my dad is running unopposed. He was always the stricter, slightly boring one, but now there's no Mum to tell him to *lighten up*. Well, not in any meaningful way. She's cancelled on meeting up with me after school *three* whole times now.

I mean, *sure* – Mum's technique of getting Dad to *lighten up* often did involve quite a lot of late-night screaming when they thought I was asleep, so I'm not saying the system was perfect.

But still. I don't get to ever bandy around dramatic phrases like, "Mum lets me!" or throw any kind of parental-competition protests in his face at all. It seems like a waste not to be able to play them off against each other.

Don't get me wrong. I didn't *want* divorced parents.

But if I'm going to *have* divorced parents, I *at least* want them to vie for my affection with material possessions in an unhealthy way that cheapens us all. Is that too much to ask?

I mean, I *don't* really want that. I want to be in Jas's family, and think they should adopt me. Though they speak about four different languages, and honestly I'm not sure I'm bright enough. But if I can't have *that*, material possessions would be the next best thing.

OK, so, just to clarify. First choice: my parents together and happy and being nice to me. Second choice: to be adopted by Jas's family, even if I have to learn Tamil and Hindi. Third choice: divorced parents desperately fighting for my attention in increasingly dehumanising and unsound ways. Simple.

Look, I said I wasn't going to get into it. Anyway, *swimming*. Everything is OK when you're swimming.

∞∞∞∞

"Watch it!" Olivia snaps, as I nearly walk into her when the changing-room door swings shut.

Rude. I mean, first of all, she wasn't looking properly either, and, second of all, this is a design flaw of the door. It's not my fault swing doors are a nightmare.

"Sorry," I say automatically. Then we both step sideways in the same direction and block each other from moving again.

Olivia sighs loudly and makes a show of holding the door open for us. So now Jas and I have to squish gratefully into the bottlenecked entrance of the girls' changing room, with all of Olivia's friends sneering at us.

"Um, thanks," I venture humbly.

It annoys me that Olivia Jones sometimes makes me flustered. She's just not *that* great. I mean, sure, she has beauty, poise and charisma, but... Well, so she's pretty great in *those* ways I suppose. But she's not got... Well, she's not very *nice*. (Yeah, so I need to work on my burns.)

Olivia and her friends all have their hair up in impressive post-swim topknots that I can never do properly. They look like elegant denim-clad ballerinas. (I'm not *against* skinny jeans or anything, but after swimming they're not exactly *easy* to put damp legs into.)

The trouble is now none of us can move. "I didn't know you *swam*," Olivia says in that weirdly

patronising way of hers.

"Well, now you do," says Jas, deadpan.

Jas is much cooler than me in a crisis. Not that this is a crisis. Yet.

"Um… Sorry, can we squeeze past?" I start trying to edge past the denim ballerinas.

"*Good* for you," Olivia enthuses to us in a fake manner. "Are you two here for the *kids'* bit?"

"Kids' bit?" I query, as no one is moving for us. "It's free swim."

"Yeah," agrees Olivia. "See, we were just in the *adult* swim session, swimming proper lengths and everything. I think they're taking away the lanes and putting out all the mats and floats now, for *all the children*, if *that's* the bit you like."

"Yes it is, *actually*," I say defiantly. I sense Jas wishes I hadn't said this.

Olivia smiles triumphantly. There's mild tittering from the others.

"Lovely!" she enthuses. "Well, we'd better be going." Then, spying my feet, she adds, "Oh, are those new shoes, Ella?"

"Um, yes."

"Nice. They suit you. Very plain." Her friends

laugh. Olivia jokily hits one of them – as if insulting me was the very *last* thing she wanted to do, and she can't *believe* she's been misinterpreted that way. "No, I mean, it's good to just stick with what you know, isn't it?" She smiles again. "Not everyone wants or can afford fashionable shoes. It's good that Ella *knows who she is*." Her smile turns into a mean smirk. "Bye, then. Have fun with the kids!" They push past us and walk off giggling.

Yet again, the joke's on *her* because I actually have *no idea* who I am. So, ha! OK, that might not be that good a sign actually.

Who *am* I? I could be anyone. I mean, sure, on the surface it looks like I'm probably a bad-shoe-wearing nerd with no confidence and an absent mum. But don't fence me in. I could be *anyone.* *

* OK, maybe not just anyone.

CHAPTER TWO

"No running!" a lifeguard shouts at Mark Sanders and Liam Stone. They ignore him and leap into the pool, making Gemma Fitzgerald laugh.

Ugh. I *hate* it when those guys are here. The three of them are in our year at school, and ages ago, in Year Seven, Jas and I nicknamed them the "Naughty Kids". Then we realised we weren't the best at making up nicknames, so we updated it to "BUTTS", which stands for Bad Unruly Tedious Twitty Show-offs.

We were quite pleased with that but thought we could still probably top it, until we realised that actually we really needed to finish our maths homework and then we never went back to it. And BUTTS grew on us. (Ahaha. Plus we liked the fun of calling them after bums.)

"Ugh, BUTTS are here," says Jas and we both smirk, pleased at our previous hilarity.

Jas and I are funny, but we're only *secretly* funny. And mostly just to each other. We don't often say stuff out loud to other people and risk a reaction. Sometimes we're funny with our friends Kaya and Debbie. And to be fair, Jas is quite good at being sarcastic, while I'm the one who tends to get more tongue-tied. But we're both a bit shy generally.

Mark and Liam proceed to have a splashing fight, which luckily doesn't reach us. Calling them BUTTS really does help alleviate the annoyance caused by whatever stupid thing they've just done.

But they are *really* infuriating in the pool. SO splashy. I always sigh inwardly whenever I see that they're here. At school sometimes they're funny, but mainly they're kind of troublesome and loud. And they're *always* messing about.

A different, neater kind of splash further away catches my attention. Someone has done a graceful dive into the deep diving pool that sits next to the regular swimming pool. I shiver involuntarily.

Jas notices. "Fancy jumping off the high board today?" she grins.

"*Hell* no," I reply.

The whole idea terrifies me. More than spiders. Or that dream where I turn up for school naked and get chased by a wolf round the canteen. (We've all had it – don't pretend you've never had the naked-wolf-school-canteen-chase dream. Just me? I mean, yeah, *me neither.*)

Jas chuckles and we turn our attention back to practising our underwater handstands. We're both really good at them now. And we can do forward rolls in the water too. I wonder if Olivia and her friends ever practise underwater handstands?

"Do you think we *are* immature for our age?" I ask Jas.

Just then, Mark suddenly does a running bomb into the pool near us, splashing water everywhere, and the lifeguard blows a whistle. *Eurgh.* Idiots.

"Nah," Jas smiles. "Well, we're not *that* immature. You know, comparatively."

I grin back at her.

We hear the lifeguard shouting at Mark. "There are little children around! Be sensible! Final warning!"

"You're not actually *bothered* by Olivia Snootypants, are you?" Jas asks me then.

"Of course not," I lie. "Well, maybe a bit."

Gemma and Liam jump off the side while attempting to fist-bump. They're really close. A mini tsunami pummels us.

"Oi!" I hear myself shout. The lifeguard's whistle blows again.

"Oh, *sorry,* Miss Goody Two Shoes!" Gemma smirks at me.

I *hate* BUTTS at the pool.

The lifeguard comes over and says something to her.

"We did look!" Gemma shrieks. "You're all right, aren't you?" she yells at a nearby seven-year-old as proof. "Fine. SORRY!" she yells at the seven-year-old again.

"Anyway." Jas rolls her eyes. "Who cares what she thinks?"

"Who?" I ask, confused. "Gemma? Or Olivia?"

"Well, both. Either." Jas hops from one foot to the other to keep warm. "Ella, this might not be 'adult swimming', but there's still lanes open in the pool now and we do sometimes do boring, normal swimming too," she elaborates. "Plus I like it when

14

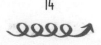

we practise somersaults and see if we can swim a width underwater." (Spoiler: we can.)

"Me too!" I agree emphatically.

And I mean it. I mean, I *mainly* mean it. But. Why can't I practise underwater handstands *and* have amazing shoes?

Dad jumps as I enter the kitchen through the back door that evening. He's sitting at the table staring into the middle distance. Alexa is playing Radio 4.

"Oh hello. Just tidying up." He puts a piece of newspaper on top of another bit of newspaper. "Your washing is on your bed. Why don't you put it away and then I'll put the crumpets on?"

"Sure."

On Sundays we always have buttered crumpets with cheese, a cup of tea and an apple for dinner.

I go upstairs, put all my clothes away and take off my new shoes. I sit on the bed and sigh.

I hate how these stupid plain shoes look. They're so *boring*. I'm thirteen now. Year Eight has already proven to be a serious business. We get to sit on *chairs* for our year assemblies now (as long as we get them out and put them away again sensibly –

still counts).

There was this one time when Mark and the rest of BUTTS got us all banned from chairs for two weeks by trying to turn them into a pyramid... *Anyway*. I should definitely be allowed to express myself through clothes more. I feel like everything I have is boring and I'm sick of it. My dad doesn't want colour on my shoes? Well, *tough luck*.

I get my Tippex out of my pencil case and draw a tiny little line roughly where a *Jay-Shees* label would be. Then, when it's dry, I colour it in red with a felt-tip pen.

This is the perfect crime. I'll wear them to school and back like this, then, when my dad doesn't notice, I'll say "Aha! Busted! The red doesn't matter. You didn't even notice. Let's go back and get my proper shoes."

I'm a genius.*

May not be an actual genius.

CHAPTER THREE

Hahahaha! (Imagine that as an evil cackle.) My dad hasn't noticed! I *knew* it! I'm at school and he didn't spot a thing. Nothing can stop me now! I can't *wait* to rub it in his face tonight. I wonder if we'll have time to go back to the shoe shop after school…? I'm weirdly excited. I love feeling like I have a secret up my sleeve. Everything suddenly seems less boring.

Jas and I are in Mrs Allison's form, 8A. We sit on a desk of four with our friends Debbie and Kaya. Mrs Allison is fine but kind of boring and seems uninterested in us. Not just us four, everyone in her form. Everyone is *quite* good for her, but no one is really scared of her or anything.

Everyone *is* scared of Miss Gaskew, our terrifying head of year. We couldn't believe it when we heard she'd be the new head of Year Eight. Her reputation as this really strict, mean monster preceded her. She *hates* the lower school and only enjoys teaching GCSE Physics.

There's actually not that many people in Year Eight or Nine, because our school, St Joseph's, got put into Special Measures by Ofsted. But my dad said, after we had looked round the school, that he thought that was probably unfair as there didn't seem to be anything wrong with it, and that Ofsted is quite a flawed way of rating schools. Mum didn't come because she'd had to take Nana Pearl to hospital again. Anyway, we're out of Special Measures now, so there's way more Year Sevens.

"Oh, hi, Jas!" I leap on to her desk in the form room and sit cross-legged, displaying my shoes. "Notice anything different about me?"

Jas puts down her phone sceptically. "Um…" She pauses. "No?"

"Exactly," I say triumphantly. "*Exactly*." I move my legs around and wiggle my toes.

"OK, you're being weird," says Jas.

"I've always said you was weird," says Debbie. Our other friend Kaya and Jas both laugh. The four of us sit together in some of our lessons too.

Olivia and her friends are being noisy in the background. I think I can make out some mild exclamations and shrieking along the lines of "oh my god", but I don't pay any attention.

"Well," I begin happily, delighted I can do my big reveal, "what it is, is—"

"Oh my *god*!" Olivia's screech just got louder and it feels like it might be directed at us. *Me*.

Ignore it.

"Anyway," I continue.

"Is that…? I think it *is*!" Olivia stands up and takes a step towards me, squinting. "Oh no, I don't *believe* it." She addresses her friends, who are looking at her, confused.

"Anyway…" I attempt again. I'm starting to feel quite uncomfortable.

"Oh, this is *tragic*!" Olivia shouts gleefully. "You guys –" she pauses dramatically – "Ella has *drawn* on her rubbish shoes to try to make them look like *Jay-Shees*!"

OK, I may not be *such* a genius.

They're coming over. Of course they are. Olivia's friends circle me, shrieking with laughter and pointing at my feet. Everyone nearby stops what they're doing and stares. I'm not going to lie: this feels like a low point.

"So weird," giggles Olivia's friend, Sasha.

"It doesn't look very convincing," says Olivia's friend, Grace. "You can totally tell they're not real."

People at nearby desks strain to look at my shoes, smirking at each other.

"Look, I wasn't trying to make them look real," I explain crossly. "I was trying to make a point to my dad."

"Ah, let's leave her alone," says Olivia finally. "It's not her fault she's the *opposite of cool*." They giggle.

"And then some," mutters Sasha.

"Look, let's just live by this rule of thumb," proclaims Olivia. "Don't do whatever Ella's doing, and you should be fine." Her friends laugh and they all walk off back to their desks.

"Well, that was embarrassing for you," says Debbie.

The rest of my day passes in a blur of feeling mortified but annoyed as I decide I will construct a list of enemies. Olivia is the only one on the list. But who says you can't have a *one-person* list? I mean, even the Count of Monte Cristo had to start somewhere.

Yes, that *was* a casual Count of Monte Cristo reference, thanks for noticing. That's right, the one from the famous story about revenge. Have you read it too?

OK, look, full disclosure: I haven't actually read *The Count of Monte Cristo*. It's *looooong*. But I have listened to some of it on audio book. Then I had to give it back. Well, I mean it automatically un-downloaded back from my BorrowBox app, because I forgot to renew it. But, you know, I got the *gist*. I think.

I suppose this is as good a time as any to mention that I am a card-carrying member of the library. (Because that's how libraries work. They don't let you take books out without a library card. I never understand why people describe themselves as card-carrying members of things they don't need cards for.)

So yes. That's right, Jas and I are also geeky *nerds*, and we *like* going to the library. We don't go on about it loads, because, you know, our school was in Special Measures and we got a sense that there wasn't much of a *Count of Monte Cristo* vibe about the place. We're not *idiots*.

But I do love the library. Jas and I have taken out books on hypnotism (turns out we *couldn't* hypnotise each other); body language (if you point your feet at someone, it means you fancy them – sounds mad, but apparently it's true because it was in a *book*); and biology (did you know, the platypus is a mammal BUT it lays eggs?! What the hell is going on *there*?!).

So, anyway. I now officially have a list of enemies, and Olivia is top of the list. I *hate* Olivia. I used to just try to avoid her, but now I want to actively *get* her. I don't know *how*, though.

The Count of Monte Cristo inherited a massive fortune off this old bloke he made friends with in the prison he was wrongfully sent to. That just doesn't feel like the type of thing that happens in Peston.

For one thing, my town is inland, so even if someone told me where their secret fortune on a tiny island was, the chances are I wouldn't very easily be able to find it. And, for another thing, there are no rich benefactors in Peston. Our town's motto is "Try Again". (They dress it up in fancy Latin, *Iterum conare*, but it doesn't exactly instil confidence.)

22

But still, I'll show her. She will *rue* the day she crossed me. Rue and lament it!

"Cheer up," says Jas, as we walk out of the school front gates and continue on to the street through the throng of pupils and parked cars. "Come back to mine – I'll get my mum to make us chocolate milkshakes?"

"That sounds – oh—" Holy … Soap Opera. I stop dead, unable to find my voice. "That's … my –" Jas stops next to me, looking concerned – "*Mum*."

There, on the other side of the street, just standing there, apparently waiting, is my mum. What the *hell*? I can't believe it.

My mum waves at me from across the street. Timidly at first, then more grandly.

"Oh, yeah," says Jas, surprised. She glances at me and opts not to wave back either.

Mum looks exactly the same as she always did: same thick black hair tied back in a ponytail; same red lipstick and dangly gold hoop earrings; same long beige trench coat.

I thought she left because she was meant to be *finding herself*? She can't even find a different coat.

It's like she's not even trying. I mean, experiment with a perm or something?

How is this more important than me? I want to scream. *This abject, continuing same-ness?* It makes a mockery of the whole "going on a journey" excuse for leaving. I mean, *obviously* the sooner my mum gets a new coat, the sooner she can come back. Or have me back. *Whatever.* Anyway, I'm pretty sure that's how this works.

"Ella!" My mum starts calling and waving. "*Ella!*"

Something twists, then loosens in my stomach and I'm suddenly worried I might cry. I can't quite find my voice.

"Ella? Are you OK? What do you want me to do?" Jas whispers.

Mum crosses the road and approaches us. "Ella, I've missed you so much!" she gushes. "I'm sorry I didn't let you know I was coming. I thought I'd surprise you! Is that OK? Hi, Jas."

The old familiar smell of her washes over me. It would be comforting if I wasn't feeling so jilted: *She hasn't even changed her perfume?* Outrageous.

"Hi," says Jas carefully.

"I've missed you so much," Mum repeats. "I can't

24

tell what you're thinking. What are you thinking?"

I'm thinking: If I burst into tears outside my school gates, are my peers more likely to assume I am:

(a) Cool and interesting, with darkly mysterious problems?

(b) Insane and laughable, and an ugly crier?

"I'm sorry," continues my mum. "I wanted to see you; it's been…" She trails off. "Hard," she finishes. "But I'm free now! Shall we do something? I have to be somewhere at eight, but—"

"No," I hear myself say.

What? This seems like a bold move for someone like me.

"No?" Mum clearly wasn't expecting that.

"I'm very busy too," I elaborate. "I have plans with Jas."

I am not just a *toy* that Mum can pick up and put down whenever she feels like it. I am a person. A human person.

"Plans?" queries Mum.

"Big milkshake plans. It's been in my diary for longer than five seconds, and when I make a commitment I stick to it," I say pointedly.

"Oh. OK," says Mum. "I'm really sorry, Ella.

How about… I'll come next Monday after school? Mondays are good for me. Usually. Unless – anyway … until eight."

"Well." I still sound weirdly cocky. "OK. Thanks. That would be lovely."

"Ella has had a bit of a shock, Mum," Jas explains as we sit at her kitchen table and Jas empties her family's biscuit tin on to a plate in front of me. They always seem to have really awesome biscuits, often *Jammie Dodgers*. "So please can you make us a cup of tea or a chocolate milkshake?"

Well, I don't know about a *shock* exactly, but I am *full* of adrenaline. I can't believe my own nerve telling my mum off like that. And, technically I lied: we'd only had our milkshake plan for exactly five seconds.

"Oh dear, what happened?" asks Deepa, Jas's mum.

"She can't talk about it yet because she's still processing it," says Jas.

"Of course," says Deepa respectfully. I can't tell if she is much nicer than every other adult I know, or if she just isn't taking the apparent crisis of a thirteen-year-old *that* seriously. "What would you like?"

"Please may I have a chocolate milkshake?" I say in a small voice.

"And, Mum? Please can you make us a proper one in the blender with real ice cream?" asks Jas.

"OK, I'll do a *proper* one." Deepa smiles, as if these demands are adorable and faintly amusing, rather than a massive faff for her. My dad almost never uses our blender, as he thinks it's not worth how fiddly it is to wash it up afterwards.

"Thanks, Mum," says Jas, and they briefly beam at each other. For about the millionth time I wish I was Jas's sister and this was my wonderful family.

"You're in shock; you need sugar," says Jas, handing me a chocolate bourbon. I thank her and start nibbling it. No Jammie Dodgers today. I'll definitely add them to the shopping list when they adopt me.

"Hey, Mum, how come you're making them chocolate milkshakes?" Jas's brother, Nav enters the kitchen. He is two years older than us and is the brashest of Jas's brothers. Her oldest brother, Manu, is four years older than us, but quite shy and quiet.

"Do you want some as well?" asks Deepa.

"Yes please." He sits down at the kitchen table, then yells over his shoulder. "Hey, Mum's making chocolate milkshakes in here! *Proper!*"

"No yelling!" yells Jas's dad, Ajith, crossly entering the kitchen.

"You're yelling," says Nav.

"I never yell," replies Ajith. Then he and Deepa talk in (I'm assuming) Tamil to each other, except the word "proper", which is in English, and then they both chuckle and look at us affectionately.

I assume they're speaking Tamil because that's the language they speak the most. I think I remember Jas telling me that in the part of India her dad is from they had to learn Hindi at school, but they preferred speaking in Tamil. I should pay more attention. I'll probably need to know this if there's an adoption exam.

"Ella, is it true you put Tippex on your shoes to make them look like *Jay-Shees*?" Nav asks me.

How does *his* year know about it? That's so unfair. "Um, no. Maybe," I say defensively.

"Why did you deface your shoes?" Ajith asks me, sitting down at the table as well.

"Um. I don't like them, I suppose," I say.

"Nonsense!" he responds grandly. "You are very lucky to have shoes!"

"Oh no, here we go," says Jas.

"*When I was a boy in India.*" Nav does an impression of his dad.

"When I was a boy in India," echoes Ajith, either not realising or not caring that he is being mocked by his family.

"Let me guess, you were very poor and you couldn't afford shoes?" suggests Nav.

"I *was* very poor growing up," agrees Ajith.

"My turn to guess," says Jas. "You couldn't afford shoes, so you had to train yourself to just float along the ground or something?"

Everyone bursts out laughing, including Ajith. "I got very good at floating," he laughs.

"Called it," says Jas.

"No, look, *of course* I could afford *shoes*," says Ajith then. "How do you think I went to medical school with no shoes on? My point is I *appreciated* my shoes."

Nav groans and rolls his eyes back in his head. "Oh, *that* was the lesson."

Deepa turns on the blender, momentarily silencing

our discussion. She starts pouring out the milkshakes into glasses. "Does Manu want some?" she asks.

"I shouted and he didn't come, so no," decides Nav. "More for us."

"He is upstairs studying," says Ajith. "He is sensible; he doesn't want a silly chocolate milkshake so soon before dinner."

"Are you having some, Dad?" asks Nav.

"Yes," replies Ajith. Everyone laughs again. "I am old now. It doesn't matter if I am silly," he explains.

I let the soothing noise of Jas's family chatting and laughing wash over me, as I drink the delicious chocolate milkshake. Somehow I feel warmed, even though this drink has real ice cream in it.

I feel much better as I finally say goodbye to Jas, and head home to my single-parent family. I wonder idly if the Chandrasekhars would maybe let my dad live above the garage or something once they've adopted me, so he doesn't get too lonely?

CHAPTER FOUR

"Hello, Ella!" says Dad jovially, arriving home from work. Then, "*Alexa!* Radio Four."

"Hi," I reply despondently.

"Oh, you look a bit sad. *Alexa!* Volume down."

"Dad, you don't need to *shout* at Alexa. She hears you at normal volume."

"Sorry, I'm having trouble understanding—"

"Alexa, off!" I snap crossly.

Dad takes off his shoes and stacks them carefully by the back door. Dad works in an office where the council process … whatever boring stuff they have to process. (He has explained it to me, but it's kind of forgettable.) He seems to neither like nor dislike his job, and on Fridays they take it in turns to bring in cake.

Dad puts his keys and bag on the kitchen table, where I have been vaguely "doing homework" but really just sort of staring mindlessly at my phone.

"What up, dawg?" he asks jovially.

"Never say that again," I instruct him irritably. Why don't parents ever realise how uncool they are? The time for them to use urban slang is *over*. Ironically or otherwise. Where did he even *hear* that? Certainly not on *Gardeners' World*.

"Mum turned up at my school today and ... wanted to hang out."

"Oh," says Dad carefully. "Well, that's *good*...?" he guesses. "Isn't it...? You wanted to ... see her more?"

Live with her. I wanted to live with her. I wanted her to *want* to live with me. I don't want to just *see* her like some visiting second cousin twice removed.

Can't say that out loud without offending the one parent who still wants me. I suddenly want to cry again.

"Hmmm," I manage.

"I'm sorry, Ella," says Dad. (I don't need my body

language book to tell me Dad looks uncomfortable.) "I don't know what to say," he continues. "I find it a bit difficult to discuss … the d— Well, the … your mother."

To be fair, my dad finds it difficult to discuss *anything*. I think that's where I get it from. His stiff upper lip is practically petrified. I know it's not his fault really. But he could *at least* offer to make me a chocolate milkshake. *Proper*.

Later, on my bed, I realise I have been zoned out thinking about Mum and have scraped all the Tippex off my shoes without rubbing in my dad's face how no one noticed about the red, and thus his point had been empirically disproven, so *ha*, he should buy me good shoes. I guess I just wasn't in the mood – the red *did* get noticed, and not in a good way. I wonder if I'll get sarcastic comments about where my fancy *Jay-Shees* labels have gone tomorrow?

Eurgh. I can't face it. It's all so pointless. I lie back on my bed and spy my trainers in the corner of the room. *Hmmmmm*. Should I? We're not supposed to. But where has toeing the line ever got me? Bullied, essentially.

Maybe it's time to see what kind of rebel* I would make.

* May not be an actual rebel.

CHAPTER FIVE

In your face, Dad, I'm wearing *trainers* to school. Ha. No one can taunt me now.

"Ella Hudson!" Miss Gaskew, our terrifying head of year, shouts across the entrance hall. "Why on *earth* are you wearing non-regulation trainers instead of proper school shoes?"

I stop in my tracks as pupils file past me, heading to their form rooms for morning registration. Miss Gaskew approaches. It feels like she's there in two strides. Everyone streaming in suddenly gives us a wide berth. *I'm not afraid of you. I'm not afraid of you*, I try to tell myself.

Come on, Ella, just like we practised in the mirror. "I lost my … my … sprained ankle!" I stammer, much more nervously than I'd intended.

"Well, which is it? You've lost your proper shoes or you've sprained your ankle?"

"My … ankle," I decide. "It's very painful. My doctor says I need the support of these comfy trainers until it heals."

"I see," says Miss Gaskew. "And I trust you have a note from said doctor to back up this fanciful assertion?"

Fanciful?

"Well, I…" Should I pretend to rummage in my bag? Ahh, I've paused too long. "I think I forgot it."

"You *think* you forgot it?"

Ummmmm. Run with it. "Yes."

OK, I am a pretty terrible rebel it turns out. I'm too nervous to lie properly.

"Well, if you're wearing them tomorrow, you can remember it and bring it to me in my office first thing before registration. Otherwise you'll be joining me in detention."

OK, the trainers thing has definitely attracted more attention than I anticipated.

"Oh, look, Miss Goody Two Shoes broke a rule," says Liam from BUTTS, as I enter the form room. Of course the irony is I no longer have "goody" shoes, so that nickname falls apart, but I opt not to point this out.

"I can't believe your nerve!" says Debbie, as I sit hotly at our form-room desks.

"Have you got detention?" asks Kaya. "I saw you with Miss Gaskew."

"Only if I wear them again tomorrow and don't bring a doctor's note," I explain.

"Wow, must be because it was a first offence," says Debbie.

Jas smiles at me reassuringly and doesn't pass judgement on my trainers. I think she thinks I'm acting out because I'm traumatised by my mum being unreliable or whatever. She's so wrong. I didn't even cry. I'm bottling everything up like a pro.

"So *I'm* writing everything down for the group?" asks Tim Rogers. (Tim is a fellow nerd.)

We have PSHCE first thing on a Tuesday morning. Mrs Allison has assigned random groups. Jas, Tim and I have been forced to join Olivia, Grace and Sasha. We're supposed to debate the possible pros and cons of the death penalty and make two columns

in marker pen on this big piece of paper we've been given.

"Great. It's not deaf," says Olivia dismissively. Sasha and Grace chuckle.

We don't get marked on our debates so Olivia never takes it seriously and lets – or rather *makes* – whoever is in her group do all the work, so her and her friends can just talk.

"Chop-chop," instructs Olivia in her patronising way. Grace and Sasha chuckle again. Then they go back to their conversation. Which, in this instance, seems to be mainly about how much fun they had at the cinema at the weekend.

"It's supposedly a deterrent," I say to get the ball rolling.

Tim writes that down in the pro column.

"Except it isn't, is it?" says Jas. "America has the death penalty, and the highest rate of murder in the world or something."

"Isn't that because they all have guns, though?" says Tim. "Plus I've written it now."

"OK," I say. "Put 'not a good deterrent, e.g. America' in the cons column."

"So we have deterrent *and* not a good deterrent?"

"She's funny," Liam concurs, addressing Mark and Gemma. (Why do they keep talking about me as though I'm not here, even though I'm *right here*?)

"That was funny earlier today," agrees Gemma. "Olivia was well annoyed."

They all chuckle in remembrance and I allow myself to join in the chuckling, feeling like I might have just grown a foot taller. I *love* the feeling that I was funny. And BUTTS are sometimes funny when they're not being disgusting, so they would know.

"Yeah!" Mark grins. He runs a hand through his hair and catches my eye. My heart jumps for a second, like I shouldn't have been looking at him right then, but that's ridiculous.

I deliberately look away. What's going on? I obviously *don't* fancy him or anything.

I mean, come *on*: I once watched him down a carton of milk that was two days past its sell-by date, then burp the word "legend" to rapturous applause from the idiots who had dared him to.

He's annoying and gross, with his dark hair that just flops in his eyes, which are a surprising shade of blue for someone with such dark hair. And his cheeky grin, and carefree sense of humour. *Uh-oh.*

inquisitive expression on his face.

I feel a mad urge to say something very impressive. Except I don't have any good pranks. *Hmm… Have I?* Ummm…

"I once locked my dad out of his car," I tell them. (I don't add that it was a total accident and I felt terrible.) I thought he had the key and I was being super-helpful by pre-locking it. But he'd left the key on the seat when he was getting his bag out of the boot and – anyway. BUTTS chuckle appreciatively, so I elaborate. "He had to smash a window, and then get a new window from a scrapyard, and get his friend Mike to help him replace it."

"Ha, brilliant," says Liam.

"Yeah," I lie.

I'm really not much of a prankster. Jas and I do *sometimes* watch prank videos on YouTube. Some of them are really funny, but then others seem kind of disgusting, and a bit mean. And sometimes I feel sorry for the person being pranked, which I know is not the point of them.

"Nice," agrees Gemma, grinning.

"That's funny." Mark smiles at me again and I beam back.

me as well.

I nod back, confused.

"This your first detention?" asks Liam. I nod again. "OK." He pauses. "The rule is, at everyone's first detention they have to burp really loudly instead of answering their name."

Gemma and Mark burst out laughing. "Don't listen to him," says Mark. "That isn't a thing."

"And it never will be with you around," replies Liam crossly.

"She wouldn't have done it," Mark tells Liam, then smiles at me kindly.

I smile back.

Wait, *what*? BUTTS aren't kind. They don't *smile kindly*.

"She would have – *look at her*," argues Liam.

See? Liam is very unkind. (And anyway, am I supposed to just pretend I can't hear them talk about me right in front of me?)

"Face it, Liam, your pranks are rubbish," says Gemma.

"Shut up. They're better than *yours*."

"You're both rubbish," Mark tells them. "You got any good pranks?" He addresses me with an

CHAPTER ELEVEN

I survey the after-school-detention crowd I find myself queuing with in the corridor.

There's four Year Nine boys that I saw having a water fight yesterday; two bored-looking Year Ten girls; a terrified-looking Year Seven boy (who is either very nervous or needs a wee because he is really shaking one leg); then Gemma, Mark and Liam from BUTTS.

"All right?" Gemma nods at me as I accidentally make eye contact with her.

Wait, *what*? She didn't call me "gomer" or "Miss Goody Two Shoes". Hang on… I stop averting my eyes and look back at her. "All right?" I reply carefully.

"S'up?" Mark and Liam nod non-committally at

against Olivia. Though she's almost definitely going to retaliate, and I haven't exactly made her rue and lament the day she crossed me. But *still*. It's an encouraging start.

And get this: I was *funny*. I'm funny now.*

* May not be that funny.

terrible disease they clearly have." They turn and head back to their desks.

Everyone else who was eavesdropping goes back to what they were doing as well. The room is suddenly buzzing with activity and conversations again.

"Um. What just happened?" I ask Jas, who is staring at me.

"You just bested Olivia in a word duel," she says.

"I *did*, didn't I?"

"How did you do that?" asks Debbie, who is also staring at me. As is Kaya.

How *did* I do that? It seems important I should know in case I ever need to do it again.

"That was great," says Kaya. "Ha."

Yeah. *Ha*. It *was* great, wasn't it? I just bested Olivia. A *bit*. I mean, let's not get *carried away*. She still got in a parting shot.

A lame one. That no one laughed at, says a voice in my head smugly. *Everyone laughed at what I said.*

Well, they tittered, I correct the voice.

What's a titter if not a laugh?

Well, a mild laugh.

A mild laugh is still a laugh.

I must be one step closer to my revenge plan

summarises Tim.

"I still can't believe that guy at the counter gave me *free* popcorn just because he thought I was *really* pretty!" says Olivia.

"I know!" gushes Sasha.

Oh *please*. Jas and I exchange a look and roll our eyes. I try not to giggle.

"No take-backs," says Jas, forcing herself to return to the matter at hand. "If you later get proven innocent. That's a con." She points for Tim to write it down.

"And I was like, *oh my god*, I can't *believe* you're giving me *free popcorn*, just because you think I'm *pretty*!" Olivia repeats.

Jas looks at me, then pulls a funny face and flutters her eyelashes to mock Olivia.

I accidentally laugh.

Olivia's head suddenly whips round to me. "What's so funny?" she queries.

"Nothing," I say quickly. "The death penalty is, uh… So you had fun at the cinema then?"

"*Um*, if you don't mind, this is a *private* conversation," Olivia replies haughtily.

Sasha and Grace stare at us like we are the height

of rudeness, even though they must *know* that sound travels when you are literally sitting next to someone. And anyway *they* are the *real* height of rudeness for making *us* do all the work.

"But actually yes, we did," says Olivia. "We saw *The Grave Robber's Hand*. Have you seen it?"

The Grave Robber's Hand is very "cool" right now. It's meant to be really scary, but in a fun way. And it's got that actor everyone fancies from that vampire movie in it.

"No," I reply.

"Of course not," says Olivia. "Why did I think you would?"

"That's a fifteen-certificate film," says Tim.

"Yeah?" agrees Olivia, seeming nonplussed.

"Didn't your parents mind?" he elaborates.

Olivia smirks at her friends and doesn't even deign to answer him.

"How did you get in?" I ask.

"Um, it's called *make-up*," retorts Olivia. "Maybe you should try it?" Sasha and Grace laugh. "And no *of course* my dad didn't *mind*. He just picked us up at ten like he's supposed to. *Duh*."

"You were allowed out at the cinema, without a

parent, until *ten p.m.*?" I blurt, surprised.

"Uh, *yeah*!" says Sasha sarcastically.

"*Duh*," adds Grace.

"Of course! It's just *embarrassing* when you get to our age if you're not," Olivia replies snidely. "But I guess, judging by those trainers, you're *used to that*."

Sasha and Grace collapse into shocked giggles, like they can't believe Olivia *went there*. Meanwhile I feel my temperature starting to rise.

"Oh just *shut up*, Olivia!" I blurt.

The three of them stop laughing and stare at me with interest.

"Leave it, Ella," says Jas.

"No, don't leave it, Ella," says Olivia. "What's she going to do? *Step* to me?"

More laughter.

"Don't give her the satisfaction of reacting," advises Tim.

I feel the familiar impotent fury cascading through my body with no proper outlet, as I don't know what to say.

Olivia stares at me expectantly. "Yes?" she prompts. "You want to say something?"

"You should just get lost!" I manage painfully. I

think even Jas winces.

They splutter laughter. "Oh bless," laughs Olivia. "Better luck next time, loser. Anyway, back to work." She taps the paper. "This boring column won't write *itself*."

And then they just go back to their cinema conversation, like nothing has even happened.

I don't contribute much for the rest of the lesson. But I have learnt two things:

(a) I really want to find a way to annoy Olivia – to be fair I knew this already.

(b) I want to go to the cinema and stay out till ten p.m. and have fun with *my* friends.

I wonder if Jas, Debbie and Kaya will want to go? I should try to set it up.

CHAPTER SIX

Maths, ugh.

"Right, I need you all to wait here quietly, while I go and get the ... other bit for this whiteboard." Mrs Williams abandons our lesson to go to the staffroom for (probably) free biscuits. I *bet* she comes back with a cup of tea.

Our class immediately (and predictably) erupts into mild chit-chat. Whenever stuff like this happens we always start off cautious, so that Mr Hilton (who is teaching maths across the hall and is MEGA grumpy) doesn't hear us, but then it nearly always escalates (usually because of BUTTS).

Jas and I are always well behaved in these situations, and so we just start playing squares in her rough book. (If you haven't played squares, it's that game where you have a grid of dots and you have to join them up, and the person who finishes the most squares wins.) I'm not saying it's the most fun ever, but it passes the time quietly and we won't get in trouble when this inevitably blows up in everyone's faces. *Squares*. I know. I get the symbolism.

The room is getting noisier around us. Some of BUTTS have already started playing catch across the room with screwed-up bits of paper. If a piece of paper hits anyone they shout "Goal!" (which is weird if you think about it, because there's no *throwing* in football. And certainly no throwing of paper. And people's heads aren't goals). Jas and I just keep our heads down (literally and figuratively).

"Oi, oi! Over here!" Across the room, Gemma Fitzgerald stands on her desk and puts her arms out like she's hugging someone invisible. "I'm a basketball hoop!" she shouts.

The game has spread, and half the room are now playing it, so Gemma is immediately pelted with loads of screwed-up balls of paper. She shrieks with laughter.

"WHAT ON EARTH IS GOING ON IN HERE?" Mrs Williams re-enters the room, carrying a cup of tea. (I *knew* it! I *told* you she'd come back with a cup of tea.) She stares at Gemma standing on her desk pretending to be a basketball hoop.

Gemma lowers her arms and breaks the shocked silence. "Sorry, Miss," she says, not looking even a tiny bit sorry. She's still smiling. "We was just playing physical maths, innit." Mark and Liam snort laughter and mutter *physical maths* under their breath like this is brilliant.

"Right," says Mrs Williams. "Well, I absolutely *cannot* have this kind of disruption in my classroom." Everyone else scuttles back to their desks. Gemma climbs down from hers. Mrs Williams surveys the room for a moment. "Gemma, swap places with Jasmine Chandrasekhar. You can sit next to Ella and see if she'll be a good influence on you."

"Noooooooooo!" shout Gemma, Jas and I in unison.

"Do it now, or we can resolve this in detention," says Mrs Williams.

Jas looks at me sadly, and then starts obediently packing up her things.

I can't believe it. I blink in shock, as Jas disappears across the room and Gemma Fitzgerald angrily slams her bag and books down on Jas's desk.

45

I can't *believe* we still got in trouble when we didn't *do* anything wrong. We were so good and quiet the *whole time*, and now we've been punished! What about fairness? What about justice? What about *squares*? This is an outrage!

Mrs Williams fixes the interactive whiteboard with whatever spurious part she needed from the staffroom (clue: a cup of tea and a lackadaisical attitude to *the truth*) and starts trying to teach us about triangles. It's so pointless: I already know what a triangle is.

"Oi, gomer," Gemma hisses at me.

"What?" I whisper back, trying to keep looking at the front.

She exhales loudly. "Eurgh. I can't believe I have to sit next to Miss Goody Two Shoes gomer."

So, er, a fun fact I should probably just fill you in on about Gemma: she has two nicknames for me. One is Miss Goody Two Shoes – fairly self-explanatory. The other is gomer.

From what I can ascertain, Gemma calls me "gomer" because once (*once)* in Year Seven I came top of the class in a mental arithmetic test (getting twenty out of twenty). And in a misguided attempt to encourage me, Mrs Williams announced it to everyone. Never mind about my right to privacy or that it literally only happened once, and I am not even especially good at maths.

Here we are, halfway through Year Eight, and Gemma is still calling me *gomer*. Sometimes "maths gomer" for a bit of variety. I *think* she thinks it means "nerd" (but I looked it up on Urban Dictionary and it *actually* means "annoying elderly patient"). So either words change their meaning, or Gemma thinks being good at maths is something only pensioners should do.

Gemma also seems to think I'm really up myself. Which I think is partly because in Year Seven (when this first happened, and I asked my dad how I should deal with name-calling at school) he said I should just ignore it. So now I think *she* thinks that *I* think I'm above having to deal with name-calling (which I suppose I sort of *do* think I am), but anyway it turns out it's not a particularly effective strategy.

By the way, can we all please just take a moment to congratulate me for managing to be bullied by two completely different groups of people, for two completely different reasons? I am "too perfect and posh" for Gemma and yet "too scummy and stupid" for Olivia. I am all things to all bullies. Go, me.

"Yeah, well, I didn't want to sit next to you either," I whisper back crossly. I sort of feel like I have nothing left to lose at this point.

"Oh, it speaks," comments Gemma, sounding amused. "Nice trainers by the way."

"Yeah, Miss Gaskew thinks so too," I reply.

Gemma makes a noise that sounds like a half-spluttered laugh. "What did you tell her?" she whispers. "What excuse?"

"Oh. Um. That I'd sprained my ankle and a doctor said I had to wear them."

Gemma nods appreciatively. "Nice. Classic, simple. She buy it?"

"No."

"You gonna fake a note?"

"A doctor's note?" *Hell* no. That hadn't even occurred to me. "Probably not."

"Wuss," says Gemma, and we go back to the lesson. Well, I go back to the lesson. Gemma goes back to doodling guns shooting (what I assume is meant to be) Mrs Williams.

CHAPTER SEVEN

"Girls! Are you ready?" my dad calls up the stairs. "We probably should go now!"

"Woohoo! Coming!" I yell back. Then Debbie, Kaya, Jas and I all clatter down the stairs, where my dad is waiting with his car keys in his hand.

My dad is trying to "cheer me up"! Hooray for awkward parents that would rather paper over the cracks than actually talk through anything! Now I get to go to the cinema with my friends!

Dad actually said the sentence "We'll have fun – I'm determined." Which is probably one of the least fun-inducing sentences ever, but, hey, you can't have everything.

I wonder idly if he's *more* determined to have fun than he was to change our porch light bulb. He seems to have given up on that for the moment. But as he said when I last asked him about it, it's only really a problem in winter when it's darker, so we might as well save the electricity for now.

But anyway... Woohoo! We're going to the cinema! On a Saturday! Me and my friends. I am every bit as sophisticated as Olivia. So, *ha*, in her face. (Not that I care, obviously.)

I mean, admittedly we're not going at *night* because my dad said no to that. We're going in the *afternoon*. And we're not seeing a *fifteen-certificate film* because he said no to that too. And also my dad is accompanying us the whole time. But *still*, pretty sophisticated.

"Oh, Ella, you haven't changed," says Dad when he sees me.

There might just be one small snag left.

"Oh. I thought you were joking," I say.

"No," replies Dad.

Oh *god*. I *think* my dad is actually serious about this. "You can't be serious," I attempt. My friends shift awkwardly in the hall, glancing at each other.

"Come on, Ella, we're waiting," says Dad.

"Dad, I'm fine like this," I protest crossly.

"You're not wearing that top out; it looks like a vest."

I'm wearing a white long-sleeved body, with a chequered shirt over the top. It is by far the almost-coolest thing I own. It is a tiny bit tight. It doesn't look like any vest that's been made since the Victorian era. Plus I'm also wearing jeans and trainers.

"Dad, you're being ridiculous."

"I disagree. Come on."

"Daaad. You come on. I thought you were trying to cheer me up? This is so silly."

"Well, if it's so silly, you can just do it then, can't you?"

"Dad, *seriously*," I say crossly.

I glance at Jas, who shrugs and looks away uneasily. I feel an uncomfortable wrench of guilt for her and the others waiting to see a film they are all looking forward to and watching this tense exchange they didn't sign up for.

"Do up the buttons of your shirt and then we can go," says Dad. "We're not going anywhere until you do."

"But…" I start and trail off.

Mum would let me. The phrase pops into my head from nowhere.

"We're not going anywhere until you do up your

buttons," Dad repeats.

"Dad, that's blackmail," I inform him.

"Well, it's up to you." Dad hangs his car keys back up on the peg.

"OK, OK!" Furious, I do up my buttons. I'm doing this for Jas and the others, I tell myself. It's not fair on *them* if we miss the start of the film. I can't *believe* my dad would promise to take us to the new Marvel movie, and then *not* do it over something so stupid. And petty. And wrong. My dad has way too much leverage over me. I *hate* being thirteen. It's so humiliating.

"That was great!" enthuses Debbie as we all walk out of the cinema at 6 p.m.

"Who wants pizza?" offers Dad enthusiastically. Everyone shouts "me" and "yes, please" except me. Though actually I *do* want pizza. I mean, I'm not *sulking* or anything, I'm just … no, actually I *am*. I am totally sulking. I can't help it.

I feel like Dad has belittled and humiliated me in front of all my friends. And that's what school is for. And maybe I shouldn't care that I had to do up the buttons of a shirt. Maybe it's not that big a deal.

But it's really taken the shine off my exciting adult cinema trip.

And *hello*? He's *supposed* to be cheering me up. Not reminding me how pointless me ever wanting things is. And certainly not throwing his weight around like some kind of ultimatum-wielding dictator.

"Darling, do you want pizza too?" Dad asks me as we walk past the American diner in the mall, and head over to the pizza place. "We can do anything you want. My treat, remember."

I mean, what a fascist. (I hear it.)

Look, I know my dad is technically being nice now, but I'm still annoyed.

"Um, sure," I say non-committally.

We get seated at one of the cool booth tables (which I would normally be excited by) and order two massive pizzas, a vegetarian one and a BBQ chicken one. Kaya is vegetarian, but Jas and I like the veggie pizza too, so it will all work out and we can all share.

Everyone is discussing their favourite and least favourite bits of the film but I'm not really joining in that much. I'm smiling politely whenever anyone makes eye contact, though, so as not to appear rude.

"BBQ chicken –" our waiter places one pizza down at our table – "and veg with pepperoni." He disappears before we can say anything.

"Dad, that's not right," I say.

"Hmm? What?" says Dad. "Tuck in, everyone."

"No, Dad, we ordered a vegetarian pizza, and they've put pepperoni on it."

"Oh." Dad seems nonplussed. "Does it matter?"

"Yes," I insist. "Kaya's vegetarian. And someone else might have our pizza."

Dad looks around the restaurant briefly. "I don't think so," he says.

"Dad, we need to send this pizza back; you need to tell them," I say.

"Oh, goodness no." Dad screws up his face to indicate the very idea is madness. "We're not sending it *back*. We'd have to *wait* for them to cook a whole other one. Can't Kaya just pick the bits of pepperoni off her slices?"

"Um, no, yes, sure," Kaya pipes up dutifully.

"Problem solved," concludes Dad cheerfully. "There's no need to make a *fuss*." He bites happily into a slice of pizza. The matter is closed.

I smile apologetically at Kaya. She gives me a *don't*

54

worry shrug back, but she looks a tiny bit put out. I feel bad for her. I mean, I know it's technically nice of my dad to be buying everyone pizza (free pizza!), but she really cares about animals, and I know she's grossed out by the idea of eating them. She makes the best of it, but she doesn't end up eating that much.

〜〜〜〜

"So that was fun!" says Dad jovially, hanging up his keys again, when we arrive home after dropping everyone off.

"Yeah, great," I say dully.

Dad suddenly sighs unexpectedly. "Ella, I'm really trying here. I'm sorry I made you button up your stupid shirt. You don't have to be so difficult. You *could* even say thank you."

The *audacity* of the man! "Oh yeah, *thanks* for making me feel about one centimetre tall in front of all my friends and treating me like a tiny child! *Thanks* for blackmailing and humiliating me. *Thanks* for making my vegetarian friend eat pig juice, just because you couldn't be bothered to wait five more minutes for a pizza," I snap.

"What? But I was very nice to all your friends." Dad appears bamboozled by my revelation. "I took you all to the cinema and bought everyone pizza. *And* I just dropped every single one of them home again. What's so terrible about that?"

"Well, *that* bit was nice," I concede glumly.

"Look!" Dad starts getting annoyed, then sighs again. "I'm sorry about … everything that's happening … with –" Dad goes into awkward mode once more – "everything."

He's lucky I speak "repressed parent" and can translate this as I'M SORRY WE'RE GETTING DIVORCED.

It's not his fault. It's no one's fault. It's one of those things. Except it is. It's everyone's fault. They're all idiots.

"I know it's hard," says Dad. "I… I don't know what I'm supposed to do here."

I don't know what *I'm* supposed to do here either. He doesn't understand where I'm coming from. I don't know how to make him.

Ugh, it's such a cliché. *We're a father-teen-daughter cliché.* Thirteen and already so basic.* How depressing.

* *Please don't let me be that basic.*

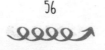

CHAPTER EIGHT

"Wow, you did it – you wore trainers again." Jas spots me in the entrance hall on Monday morning. She thought I was *bluffing* at swimming yesterday. Well, *HA*.

"Honestly, Jas," I reply blithely, as we head up together through the crowd of pupils towards the main corridor, "I'd rather be yelled at by Miss Gaskew than insulted by Olivia." (Especially until I can think of a good revenge plan.)

"Then your priorities are weird," replies Jas. "Also, Olivia totally insulted your trainers too."

"Yeah, but not as badly as my other shoes. Anyway. It's fine," I say dismissively. "Miss Gaskew probably won't even notice. I probably just got unlucky the other time."

"Ella Hudson!" Miss Gaskew shouts across the throng. We both stop and she strides towards us. "I see your ankle must be playing up again?" She raises a sceptical eyebrow and nods towards my feet. Less *HA*.

"Yes, Miss," I reply dejectedly.

"Sorry to hear it." She pretends to go along with this. "Strange, as it seemed to repair itself for much of last week. May I see your doctor's note?"

"Miss, Ella's not feeling very well, please can she just bring it tomorrow?" suggests Jas supportively.

"I'm sure Ella is quite capable of telling me this herself," replies Miss Gaskew. "Ella?"

At this moment a half-asleep wasp buzzes on to my shoulder. I jump and try to swerve it away, but, taking an unexpected step sideways, I trip and fall backwards. I end up essentially lying down in the entrance hall surrounded by everyone walking past, who – obviously – find this amusing. For a moment I close my eyes and consider not getting back up.

"That's detention," Miss Gaskew pronounces.

"Miss, there was a wasp!" cries Jas, pulling me to my feet. "Didn't you see it?"

"Wasp or not, there is no need for such *silly*

theatrics. I don't have time for people pretending to faint!"

That isn't even what happened! God, the world is stupid.

"Is it true you got detention for pretending to faint when Miss Gaskew was telling you off?" Gemma is (*unbelievably*) still sitting next to me in maths. Mrs Williams seems to think her plan to make people behave is *working*, so continued injustice prevails.

"If you like," I reply dully.

Gemma chuckles delightedly. "Wish I'd seen her stupid face!" she whispers.

I smile genuinely. Miss Gaskew's face *is* stupid. I'm glad someone is finally saying it. Even if that person is Gemma from BUTTS. Jas, Debbie and Kaya always talk about Miss Gaskew with this annoying sort of fearful, reverential hush.

"Yeah, I missed it too because I was lying on the floor with my eyes closed," I whisper. "But she was *not* happy." Gemma chortles appreciatively.

"Everything all right over here?" Mrs Williams is doing that thing where the teacher walks around the room to make sure we all work in silence. (I *bet* she's just got a new Fitbit or something.)

"Actually, Miss, Ella is feeling a bit *faint*. Could you open a window or something?" says Gemma.

A few people chuckle. But for the first time in a while it doesn't feel like it's completely *at* me. I mean, still a *bit* at me, sure, but with a little hint of an in-joke thrown in.

"Do you feel ill, Ella?" asks Mrs Williams.

"I'm fine, Miss." I smile politely and get back to my work, feeling the tiniest bit buoyed up since the weekend.

"I still can't believe they won't let you move back next to me in maths yet," I complain to Jas, as we exit the gates at the end of school. "It's so unfair."

"Oh, is that what you think?" says Jas sarcastically. "It's so hard to tell from the way *you've talked about nothing else*," she adds pointedly.

"Aren't you bothered?" I ask her.

"Of course I am, but there's not much I can do about it, so I'm not wallowing," Jas replies simply. As if it's *that easy* to just *choose* what annoys you.

"Oh!" Jas gasps suddenly. "Don't look now, but she's back."

"Wh— Oh!" My mum is standing across the street again, just like she was last Monday. *She made it!*

Mum waves timidly at me again. I pause and wave back. She starts crossing the street towards us.

"Are you *sure* you want to do this?" whispers Jas.

OK, to be fair, I confidently predicted to Jas that Mum wouldn't show, and that I was glad because I didn't want to see her anyway. I would have thought this obvious lie showed me up as protesting too much, but apparently I was convincing because Jas now thinks I really don't want to see my mum. Jas has been very kind and understanding about the whole divorce thing. Well, she's been doing her *concerned and supportive* best friend routine. Which is really nice. Definitely. But also makes me feel a bit ... not *patronised* exactly... I just don't think she really gets it.

"Yeah, it's fine. It's my mum," I tell Jas.

"OK, quickly," says Jas, "how about code word *lettuce* and I can make an excuse and grab you away? No, *elephant*. No, *lettuce*, stick with *lettuce*," she garbles before my mum meets us.

I love Jas and I appreciate this, but I also think it's a *bit* over the top.

"Hiya!" says Mum. (Still persisting with the same coat, lipstick and earrings, I see.)

"Hey," I reply.

"S'up," says Jas and we both look at her. "Sorry, I can't pull that off. Just trying it out. Also, I was trying to make it less awkward for you."

"It's not awkward!" gushes Mum incorrectly. She makes a sudden weird gesture that looks like it might be going for a hug, but then abandons it and pats my shoulder instead.

"*Phew*," says Jas, deadpan. But Mum doesn't pick up on any sarcasm.

"So!" says Mum brightly. "Can I please take you out for a delicious milkshake? I hear they're all the rage now." (*Pah*, she heard that from *me* last week when I refused to see her.)

"Um ... yea—"

Mum interrupts my answer. "Or a coffee? Or a hot chocolate? And cake? Um, Jas can come too, of course."

"What do you think, Ella?" asks Jas. "Do you want a milkshake? Or do you need to come with me and get ... *lettuce*?" Mum glances between us, a little perplexed.

"No, it's OK," I tell Jas. "I don't think I need …
lettuce."

"And do you want me to come with you now, or
should I just crack on with the *lettuce* by myself?"
continues Jas.

"It's OK, Jas. No lettuce right now," I say. "You,
er, go on without me. I'll be fine."

"Are you *sure*?" persists Jas.

"*Yes*," I insist. I'm pretty certain Mum can't crack
our secret code.

"OK. Well, text me if you change your mind, or
need … anything." Jas hoists her bag higher on to
her shoulder. "Bye."

Mum still looks a bit confused, so to cover our
subterfuge tracks further, I say enthusiastically,
"Classic Jas. She's just really into lettuce at the
moment."

"Great!" enthuses Mum. "Feels like just yesterday
to me that you two were really into cups!"

Jas and I were *really* good at cups. Still are. Full
disclosure: we did it again the other day for old times'
sake and we're still excellent.

Great. Now I have that song stuck in my head.

CHAPTER NINE

"I'm so glad we could do this!" enthuses Mum.

"Sure."

I mean, she had me at "milkshake". Or really, at just turning up when she said she would.

Mum orders me a slice of walnut cake and hot chocolate (controversial I know, going for a hot chocolate after wanging on about milkshakes, but I thought it would go better with the cake). Mum orders herself an Americano with an extra shot of coffee in it. (You'd never catch my dad having that much caffeine after 4 p.m.)

"I've missed you so much!" says Mum. "I have tried to call as often as I can. I know it's not the same. I think things are going to be much easier soon." Mum sounds earnest.

"Yeah," I agree doubtfully.

"Do you—"

"I saw—"

We both talk over each other, and then chuckle nervously. Then we argue about who gets to talk first.

"No, you go," insists Mum.

"Honestly, what I was going to say wasn't that interesting," I tell her.

"*Everything* you have to say is interesting," proclaims Mum. "And you're so beautiful."

"Thank you," I say dubiously.

"I'm so…" Mum looks uncharacteristically vulnerable. "I'm so sorry I left, Ella. I need you to know it was nothing to do with you."

Oh no. Here we go. I both *was* and *wasn't* expecting her to say that.

"I never wanted it to happen like this. You understand that, don't you? I need you to understand that."

"Sure," I reply non-committally.

Of course she *would* say that. I mean, that's just what you say, isn't it? "*It wasn't your fault.*" "*Your bum looks great in those hot pants.*" "*Thanks for the Clarks shoes, Dad.*"

"I know the drill," I say tiredly. "Not the kid's fault, yada yada yada."

"I mean it," says Mum. "It's so hard to explain to a … child. You might understand more when you're older, I guess."

"I'm actually very mature, so…" I hear myself say.

"No, of course," agrees Mum. "Well, the … the thing is, I was very young when I met your dad and had you."

"Sure," I say again.

"I never went to college. I'd never really been abroad. I mean, I know we went to the Isle of Wight that time as a family, but it's not the same thing… And I just … you know, I felt frustrated, like, what about *my* dreams, you know?"

I nod as if I understand, but I'm seriously not loving this explanation so far.

"And then, after your nana died, I just couldn't handle it any more."

Oh yes, *death*. No one's allowed to argue with that. (Poor Nana Pearl.)

"It was so hard, Ella. I just… But I realised: life is short. Shorter than we ever think. She was only fifty-six. It's like… If you're not going to do something now, when are you going to do it? You have to seize the day. Because actually, what's scarier – all those things you're afraid to try to do? Or never knowing if you could have done them?"

OK, now Mum sounds like some kind of No Fear surf-clothes advert.

"I mean, your dad thought I should just take the medication—"

Wait – the *what* now?

"But I said to them, I'm not depressed, I'm *bereaved*. I'm *heartbroken*, but pills aren't going to bring her back. And my mood swings are probably because I'm unhappy for other reasons. What if there's something I could do to make myself better, without resorting to drugs? What if I could go away and ... and just do ... the ... *missing things* ... and then come back and be a good mother again? Wouldn't that be worth a try?"

I'm still nodding, so she continues.

"I didn't want to leave you. I wasn't in a good place. I guess desperate times call for desperate measures." She sort of chuckles humourlessly. "I feel much better now. I'm nearly there." Then she looks at me earnestly. "Do you understand?"

What else can I say? "Sure."

It's probably better I say that than anything mean, isn't it? Plus maybe I'll go to bed tonight and sleep on it, and in the morning it will all make perfect sense and I really *will* understand it. I'm just playing it safe.

Mum sighs this huge sigh of relief. She looks visibly lighter. "Oh, I'm so glad!" she enthuses. "You are amazing. You really *are* mature for your age. A lot of thirteen-year-olds wouldn't have understood at all."

Ha. She's definitely not going anywhere now. She's totally happy again. And all I had to do was pretend not to have feelings. I imagine this pretence will be fairly easy to keep up. I just have to repress all my emotions. I'm pretty sure that always ends well for people…

"I'm finally using my brain now," says Mum. "I've started my own business. Can you believe it? *Me!* Property development. I can't wait to show you."

"Coffee for you." The waitress puts a cup down in front of Mum. "Hot chocolate." She places one in front of me. "And one carrot cake, with two forks."

"Sorry, no, we ordered walnut cake," says Mum.

"Oh, um, really?" says the waitress.

"Well, that's OK, we could have—" I begin.

"No," interrupts Mum. "Yes, we definitely ordered walnut cake and that's what we would like. Please can you take this back and bring us the walnut cake."

"Oh, OK." The waitress picks up the plate, looks back at the counter and winces. "I'm really sorry, but someone at the counter has just served the last piece of walnut cake over there," she says.

"Well, that sounds like a whole load of *not my problem*," says Mum breezily.

"Sorry?" says the waitress. (It sounds like our problem to me.)

"If *you* had got our order right, that would have been *our* last slice of walnut cake," says Mum. "So what are *you* going to do about it?" Mum glances at the counter and back to the waitress.

I feel myself going hot, as all Mum's other qualities come flooding back to me. Her assertiveness. Impatience. Aggression.

"Um…" says the waitress, unsure.

"I'll give you a list of options," says Mum, still breezy. She seems like she's enjoying herself. "Option one: I complain to your manager; option two: I go and harass the customer that got my cake; option three: you give us this unwanted carrot cake free of charge and we say no more about it."

"Um, well… I suppose we'd better do that one," replies the waitress, placing the carrot cake back on our table.

I don't know where to look. I feel bad for the waitress. But also … *also*, I realise, that even though I am definitely *embarrassed*, part of me is secretly sort of impressed … maybe even *thrilled* at my mum's ability to do that.

Dad and I can't do that. I can't stick up for myself. Dad can't send back the wrong food. But Mum can. And she made it look effortless. She deliberately engaged in a public confrontation, and no one died.

Maybe I need to be more like that? Maybe ignoring your problems *doesn't* make them go away?

"I can't believe you got us free cake," I say.

"The squeaky wheel gets the grease." Mum winks and sips her coffee, leaving a small amount of red lipstick on the cup. "You would not *believe* how well I've taken to running a business." Then she suddenly spies my feet. "What's with the trainers? Are you allowed to wear them to school?"

"No," I reply honestly.

And then I find myself telling my mum all about Dad not buying the *Jay-Shees*, me getting sort of bullied about it, trying to disguise my rubbish shoes, and that backfiring, and then finally wearing trainers. She's still really easy to talk to. I also somehow manage to eat all the cake. Mum doesn't even touch it.

"Well, that Olivia *whatsherface* better hope she doesn't run into *me*," says Mum. "Come on." She drains her cup and stands up, reaching for her coat off the back of her chair.

"Where are we going?" I ask. Please don't let it be to find Olivia Jones...

"Shoe shopping," reveals Mum, leaving a nice tip for the waitress.

Oh my god, oh my god, I *own* a pair of *Jay-Shees*! I'm so happy and buzzed as I enter my house later on Monday evening. Plus this will definitely help me repress my more negative emotions about Mum leaving. We're practically even again now she's got me these shoes. Even-stevens. Probably.

But anyway, I can't *believe* it! Things are finally

looking up for old Ella Hudson!

"*There you are!*" shouts a cross voice.

And then down again.

Dad appears to have been lurking, so he can catch me as soon as I get in. What kind of person *does* that? Not a well-adjusted one, that's for sure.

Dad and I haven't been getting on *brilliantly* since our sort of impasse on Saturday. We're still talking and everything. We still had our Sunday-night tea of crumpets, cheese and apples. But there's a sort of a ... *distance* I guess.

"Hello?" I reply suspiciously.

I can't help but feel that an angry "*there you are*" is rarely followed by good news. I doubt anyone has ever had cause to use the sentence: "*There you are! You've just won a Nobel Peace Prize!*" Or: "*There you are! I've just baked you your favourite biscuits, let's eat them now instead of a sensible dinner involving broccoli.*"

So I suspect I'm not going to like whatever comes next. Which is so unfair. Can't I just be allowed to be happy for *five minutes* without someone coming along and ruining it?

"I just had a phone call from the school informing

me that you missed a lunchtime detention that you were supposed to have today," says Dad.

I *knew* it! Well, I didn't know *that*. I actually completely forgot about that. Hence missing it. Whoops. But I knew this was bad news, so in a way … *called it*.

"Oh," I say.

"Oh," echoes Dad. "So now you have an after-school detention tomorrow."

"Oh *what*? That's so lame!" I blurt out.

"Why on earth were you wearing trainers in the first place?" demands Dad. "I just bought you a perfectly good pair of new school shoes."

"Well, you see the thing is, remember how I wanted the—"

"I am so disappointed in you," interrupts Dad.

"Don't worry, I won't wear the trainers again," I tell him, hoping to head off an entire lecture.

"Well, we agree on something then." Dad sighs. "Where have you been? School finished ages ago."

"I, um. OK. Well. I met up with Mum."

"*Did* you?" Dad tries to mask his reaction. "Right. Well. I suppose she did say she would…" He trails off momentarily. "That's, um … *good*? Did she turn up outside the school gates again?"

"Yes. Have you … been *in touch* with her?" I ask curiously.

"Well, of course," replies Dad. "We've had to maintain contact this whole time to make arrangements for you. It's just mainly been … a bit one-sided till now."

Well, well, well. The secret life of divorced parents. Hah. *That* would be a disappointing follow-up to *The Secret Life of Five-Year-Olds*. It would probably just be a show where middle-aged people email each other about who gets Christmas, while a psychologist concludes they are being passive aggressive.

"Um…" Dad pauses and looks uncomfortable, a sure sign he wants to say something that makes him feel awkward. "Look, I don't want to stop you seeing her or anything…" Another pause. "I'm … *delighted* she's giving you her time again."

"But?" I supply tiredly.

"But … well, I don't love the way she doesn't plan ahead, and now you've suddenly got detention. You need routine and consistency, and … *people* need to stick to the routines and consistency."

I groan inwardly. Then outwardly. I can't help

it. "Dad, I think you've confused cause and effect again," I say condescendingly. "Like that time you thought eating a whole packet of ginger biscuits was the reason you didn't get the flu last winter."

"Look, I'm sorry," says Dad, "I *do* want you to see her. And I want us all to be friends."

"I want that too," I reply.

We do a tiny lacklustre hug, then step back apart. *Why is this so weird now?*

"I'm supposed to be cross when you get detention, that's my job," explains Dad.

"I'm *never* going to be cross if *I* have a kid that gets detention," I retort. "I'm going to be really sympathetic and agree with them that the school rules are stupid."

"Well, your kid is going to be a delinquent," says Dad bluntly.

"How dare you insult my future kid!" I raise my voice angrily. "You don't know anything."

"Fine." Dad sighs wearily. "Just be careful, Ella."

Be careful. So patronising. I'll be careful all right. Careful like a *fox*.*

* *May not be that careful.*

CHAPTER TEN

Actually foxes probably do need to be quite careful, don't they? Loads of people want to kill them. Poor foxes. And they're so clever. I really like foxes. I think it's because I loved reading *Fantastic Mr Fox* when I was younger. I wonder idly whether if everyone had to read that when they were six, foxes would be a protected species by now?

"I can't believe you just *forgot* you had detention." Jas snaps me back to reality in our form room on Tuesday morning. She has a point, to be fair.

"I know!" I exclaim. "And that's what BUTTS say, and I never believe them, but I really did forget."

"Ha, you're in BUTTS now," jokes Jas.

"I'm not *in* BUTTS," I object.

"No, that would be gross," Jas laughs, then catches

my face. "Well, you've had a lot on your mind." She shifts tone and tries to be consoling. "Amazing that your mum was so open with you, though."

"Yeah," I say vaguely.

"Death is, you know ... a really *huge* thing to deal with. Makes people do all sorts of things. I read about it in that psychology book we got from the library."

I wish Jas would stop talking about it now.

"Jas, we don't need a library book to tell us death makes people *sad*," I reply tersely.

"But it doesn't *just* make them sad," protests Jas, "it makes them—"

"Yeah, yeah, leave their children, etc., etc.," I interrupt. "Let's talk about something else."

Jas looks quite taken aback. "Um, yeah, sure, stuff like that. Well, OK."

Great, now I feel bad for upsetting Jas. But honestly, I don't see why my gran dying means Mum had to leave. I'm sad *too*. I miss Nana Pearl. Why didn't her mum dying make her want to be a *better* mum to me? Why did we both have to lose our mums?

"But you, um, told your mum you were totally fine about everything?" says Jas carefully.

"Of course I did. I *am* totally fine with everything,"

I say. "Look, she got me these shoes," I wave my *Jay-Shees*-clad feet at Jas. Even-stevens.

"It *is* cool we're *shoe twins*," smiles Jas, wiggling her feet too.

Olivia enters our form room and goes to walk past me, but does a slight double take as she spies my wiggling feet. She stops and takes a step back towards me.

"No *way*," she accuses me. She looks from my shoes to my face a couple more times.

Sasha and Grace curiously wander over from their desks, possibly wondering what the hold-up is. Their presence seems to make Olivia force the shock off her face and replace it with a smirk.

"Oh. My. God." Sasha has clocked my shoes.

"Is that – are they *Jay-Shees*?" Grace follows her gaze. Kaya and Debbie finish their conversation abruptly to listen in. I start to feel a bit hot.

"Are they *real* or have you crafted them yourself out of Play-Doh and wishful thinking this time?" asks Olivia snidely. The three of them laugh.

"Not that it's *any of your business*," I say hotly, "but, yes, they're real."

"They're *real*?" Olivia frowns. I nod. "How did

you—?" She starts, sounding annoyed, then pauses. "They don't suit you. I think you should take them back."

"*What?*" Jas manages to sound both bored and cynical, which I am impressed by.

Olivia ignores her. "Come on, Ella," she says in her fake kind voice. "Those shoes are worth *a lot* of money to a povvo like you. Imagine what you could do with that money. Do yourself a favour." They all smirk at me again, though Sasha and Grace roll their eyes at each other like they think this is a bit harsh but are still impressed by Olivia's gall.

I'm kind of blindsided by the audacity and rudeness of it all. And I guess I shouldn't be. This is *Olivia* we're talking about after all. So much for the bullies leaving you alone if you fit in.

The worst part is, other people are starting to lean in and listen. The desk of four next to ours just hushed up. Even BUTTS just gathered a bit nearer. There's an *audience* now. This is horrible. What am I supposed to even *say*?

What would *Dad* say? "Olivia," I begin sternly, not sure where I'm going with this, "I'm keeping them. And I think you might have altogether too

much interest in my footwear." That probably sounds pompous. *Hmmm*. What would *Mum* say?

"I don't want you wearing the same shoes as me," says Olivia firmly.

"Really? Well –" I cast my mind around desperately – "that sounds like a whole load of *not my problem*," I retort.

Shocked titters from the surrounding audience. *At Olivia*. With *me*, AT OLIVIA. Oh my god. Shoe on other foot! (So to speak.) Sasha and Grace gasp. Olivia looks bamboozled. I just *sassed* my way to a mild victory by channelling my mum. My embarrassing shouty-in-public mum.

Olivia glares at me in abject shock before she recovers herself. She's aware of the audience. She can tell their allegiance just shifted. She's no longer enjoying this. She can't think of what to do.

"Well," says Olivia airily, "maybe the stock of *Jay-Shees* is about to *plummet* and we should all stop wearing them now that they've officially *peaked*."

Grace and Sasha chuckle dutifully but they don't look amused.

Olivia addresses them. "Come on, let's leave the copycat *wannabes*; we don't want to catch whatever

Please don't tell me I just developed a crush on Mark from BUTTS. That would be *insane*.

"Someone's coming," says Mark.

I accidentally make eye contact with him again and suddenly feel hot and sweaty, like when I get bullied, except a *bit* nicer.

"I can't hear anything," replies Liam. "Anyway –" he addresses me – "for a first detention you don't even seem upset about it."

"Not much I can do about it now is there?" I reply honestly and shrug. For some reason they seem impressed by this answer.

"Ha," says Liam. "She does not care."

"Calm," agrees Gemma.

"Right, thank you for waiting," Miss Gaskew interrupts, and opens the door to the classroom. "Let's begin, shall we?"

ᚖᚖᚖᚖ⤳

God, I'm bored. And *thirsty*. Why didn't I think to bring a bottle of water or a Capri Sun with me or something?

This is SO unfair. Stupid detention. *And* the water fountain is broken and I was 5p short of affording a can from the can machine. I should be home drinking drinks for free. Not sitting in this stupid hall just because Miss Gaskew doesn't like my trainers.

I'm sure this is a violation of my human rights. I bet there are laws against this. Why is everyone an idiot except me? I hate this. I'm so angry. I just want to leave. I can't just sit here any more. I have to *do* something.

I raise my hand. "Miss?" (What exactly am I doing?) Well, maybe I can be funny again.

"Ella?" Miss Gaskew responds tiredly, looking up.

"Please can you lend me 5p for the can machine?"

BUTTS snigger and look up to see what will happen next.

"I think you know the answer to that," responds Miss Gaskew, going back to the marking on her desk.

I decide to ride the laughs I'm getting. "Brilliant, thanks Miss," I reply. BUTTS chuckle, and some of the other kids join in.

"Do not *test* me, Ella," Miss Gaskew threatens idly. "Unless you want more detentions?"

"But, Miss, the water fountain is broken and I'm thirsty." I forget to be funny and start getting earnest and angry. "How am I supposed to drink? I'm sure the school is legally obliged to provide free water." I have no idea if this is true, but it sounds like it should be.

"Well, maybe you should have thought about that before you broke school rules."

"*What?* How could I have known the school was going to renege on its duty of care to thirsty students?"

Miss Gaskew tuts, stops marking books and looks up at me. "You may drink from the toilet for all I care."

The others laugh again, but this time *at* me. I glance at Mark, but he's not looking at me or anything. So much for being funny making me the author of my own destiny.

I go red and look down, mortified and incensed at the same time. I wish I was better at confrontations and sticking up for myself. I need to get better. I *will*.

Ugh. This is SO UNFAIR. I hate everyone. And I'm *really thirsty*. Now it's all I can think about. And I bet the school ARE meant to provide free water. Instead they're coining it in with an expensive can machine, while the company that made it doesn't even pay its proper tax.

It's like a conspiracy. Probably a global one. It's corrupt. I demand justice! I sit there seething and then I form a plan. A vigilante justice-restoring plan.

No one will ever know it was me who wrote "TAX-AVOIDING SCUM" in Tippex on our school's can machine.

CHAPTER TWELVE

Mum is waiting for me at the bus stop outside Boots on Saturday, just like we arranged.

"Hello, darling!" She squeezes me into a massive hug. She's my reliable and fun mum again, just like before. "Ready to shop till you drop?"

Well, OK, that bit's new. We never really *shopped* before. We did *activities*. Mainly. "Um, OK," I say.

"Blimey." She clocks my bag. "What's with the Crown Jewels?"

"Eh?"

"That looks heavy. What's in it?"

"Oh, well, some library books I was going to take back, and a bottle of water, and I always carry deodorant and, well, other things just in case, like sunscreen and plasters…"

Mum raises one of her perfectly shaped eyebrows. For some reason I briefly wonder if she will call me a geek.

"Never mind." Mum inspects inside my bag. "Why are all your library books hardbacks?"

"That's just what they happened to have."

"*The Diary of Adrian Mole* –" she keeps rummaging – "has been out *aeons*. That's definitely in paperback now."

"It's not my fault what the library has."

"This is the largest canister of deodorant I have ever seen! Haven't you ever heard of travel size?"

"No."

"OK. Look. I realised something the other day, in the coffee shop: I haven't really been there for you lately."

Well, *duh*. Don't get angry. Say something nice. "Well, you're here now," I offer.

"No, I mean, even before the … divorce. I was distracted. I was spending all my free time at the hospital. And then obviously I wasn't *myself* after Mum… Anyway, my point is: I never got round to showing you how to be a cool teenager! I mean, you're thirteen! It's such a fun age!"

"Is it?" (Was I meant to be having *fun* this whole time?)

"I *loved* being thirteen," gushes Mum. "Finally getting to wear make-up. Starting to go out. Getting more freedom. Getting really into fashion and music." She sighs wistfully. "When you told me about that horrible girl and your shoes, and your dad not buying them, it really brought home to me that there's this whole side of things that I've totally neglected for you."

I'm not *neglected* because Mum hasn't bought me cool shoes before. *Am I?* I mean, I do *feel* a bit neglected.

Mum continues. "I mean, I guess I *partly* never thought of it before because it always seemed like you and your dad love books and all that type of thing. I never wanted to *force* you to have the same interests as me. But actually, now you're getting older, there's room for a little bit of sparkle, *mama-style!*"

Wait, *what?* Go back one. "What do you *mean* me and Dad love books and *all that type of thing?*" (Is that Mum-code for *geek?*)

"Oh, well, you know, you and your dad both get quite engrossed doing your own thing. And I was always the noisy one, making Alexa play music too loudly instead of Radio Four, and generally annoying you both."

WHAT? "How can you think that? I was *never annoyed*. You're the fun one!" I blurt out.

"That's nice, darling. But I'm not upset or anything. He's a much better … fit for you. Especially until I'm back on my feet."

Oh great, I just happen to "fit" my more boring parent, do I? Thanks a lot. That's insane. And I mean, *who wants to live in a house without music?* Oh god, I now live in a house without music.

"Anyway." Mum beams. "Let's get you kitted out!"

"We'll take them." Mum proffers her card and smiles at me.

If the best words in the English language are officially "It's benign", followed closely by "I love you", I would like to nominate "We'll take them" as a third-place runner-up.

Health. Love. Material Possessions.

I am now the proud owner of (among other things) a really great skirt, two amazing dresses, some awesome "fashion tights", skinny jeans, some really cool tops, *and* some crazy animal slipper-socks. (Not *everything* has to be cool.)

I wonder how I didn't realise shopping could be *fun* before. I suppose Mum has a point. She did *try* to do this stuff when I was about ten, but I was too young to care and did get a bit bored and whiney. Then Nana Pearl got sick and Mum *was* quite busy with all that.

My other forays into the world of shopping have mainly involved sort of trailing around after Jas and *her* mum, sometimes trying stuff on; then watching her mum buy her stuff; then slightly spoiling their fun by whining that I'm tired and suggesting we get chips; then going home and recommending Dad buy me stuff; then Dad declining because we don't have "spare" money and, anyway, my requests weren't really "practical".

I guess *actually buying things* is quite an important part of shopping. Well, I am through the looking glass, people – I am a *shopper*.

Mum seems to have "spare" money *now*. To be fair, she is *still* a real bargain hunter. She got us money off a very posh-looking jumper because there was a thread loose and no other ones in my size; money off a really nice pair of shoes because they were an ex-display model; a few things in sales; money off some stuff at the market because we "bought in bulk" and "deserved a discount". Mum has always loved "haggling" and arguing with people to get the price down. In some ways she's lived her whole life like an overly keen *Apprentice* candidate. So it sort of does make sense to me that she's now running her own business. I *guess*.

There was one *minor* moment of mortification at the market, when a man tried to aggressively sell Mum a discount box of vinyl records, and Mum eventually said, "1971 called, it wants its stuff back!" Then she laughed in the man's face, but luckily we didn't hang around for his retort, so it didn't turn into a *scene* or anything.

There used to be a lot of *scenes* when I was younger. Dad always used to be saying, "Shhh, don't make a *scene*," and he was never talking to me.

"Right," says Mum, looking satisfied. I assume she's about to announce we are done, which would be fair enough, but instead she says, "Accessories next, then make-up."

I'm too stunned to reply and she leads me into a

trendy accessories shop. We look around a bit at all the funky wallets, bags and scarves, then Mum leads me over to the jewellery.

"Oh, we must get these bracelets for you!" she exclaims, lifting up some cool-looking bracelets and putting them on my wrist to see. They're kind of beaded, but bigger, though still small and delicate, and one is pastel-but-shiny blue, one is pastel-but-shiny pink, and one is pastel-but-shiny purple. They all have gold and silver bits running through them and are kind of mesmerising.

"These are very *in*," says Mum confidently. "In fact, I think Elisa Croft was even talking about them on her latest *Haul* vlog."

Wait, *what*? Elisa Croft the teenage YouTube star and fashion expert? Aaagghh, two worlds colliding. "How do *you* know who Elisa Croft is?" I blurt.

"I'm cool and trendy," Mum grins. "Also, I did a course on how to build a social media presence at the college. She's a good case study."

"That's a *course*?" I'm bewildered.

"A two-day one, yes," says Mum. "For homework we had to start a Facebook group and try to get likes."

"You are absolutely kidding me!"

"I'm really not," Mum laughs. "It was hilarious. I think I was the youngest person there. It was all middle-aged people trying to stay relevant in the new markets. Still, useful, though."

Mum did for *homework* what young people do for *fun*. (Or at least what young people used to do for fun before old people took over Facebook.) The world has gone upside down.

"Plus, hashtag I've finally been to college!" Mum laughs and I join in. She does seem happier than she has in a while. She's animated and proud of herself. And relaxed and laughing. Not picking fights with me or Dad.

I just can't believe Elisa Croft is in a *course*. Jas and I *sort of* like Elisa Croft, but we find her a bit annoying and perfect. We once filmed our own spoof version of "What's In My Bag?" with our school bags. I opined that I couldn't go anywhere without my old piece of chewing gum, and Jas pulled out a new sanitary towel from hers, held it to her cheek, and said straight-faced, "This is one of my favourites. I just always feel better knowing this is here." I think I laughed for about ten minutes. We never had the guts to post it online. I think it might still be on

Jas's phone.

"Anyway," Mum is saying, "They look great on you. I think we should get all three, that way you can wear them together to jazz up a plain outfit, or one at a time if you want to match another colour you're wearing."

"OK," I hear myself say. I do like these bracelets. I gently shake my wrist and admire them. They make me feel special and dressed up.

We then also get a couple of necklaces, a really nice notebook, and a funky new wallet that I can't wait to show Jas.

"*This* is the kind of bag you should have." Mum points out a sleek pink and black bag with a black and white cityscape print on one side, topped with pink glitter. "It's small when there's hardly anything in it – which should be most of the time," she says pointedly, "but can still expand if it needs to."

I examine the bag. It isn't the kind of thing I would normally go for. But it is quite cool I suppose. And it has inside pockets, which I like. "OK," I say. "You've convinced me." Mum beams and buys everything.

We stop at the American diner place inside the mall for coffee and chips. Well, I have a chocolate milkshake. It's 2 p.m. now but Mum says she's usually too busy to "do" lunch. She eats a fair few of the chips, though.

So this is shopping, I keep thinking to myself.

"This is so much fun!" I tell her happily.

"I'm having a blast too!" she beams. "Oh, hang on." She frowns as her phone buzzes. "Hang on a sec, I'll be right back." Mum walks away from the table to take her phone call.

I enjoy sitting on the high stool at our cool little circular table surrounded by shopping bags, and watch the world go by. All these people walking around the mall. I bet they're not as happy as me. I've just had all my Christmases come at once.

"Right. I'm back." Mum reappears. "I had a quick look at the cinema listings just now and was wondering if you wanted to see *The Grave Robber's Hand*?" (Oh wow! That's the cool fifteen-certificate film that Olivia and her friends saw!)

"*Really?*" I exclaim.

"The only thing is," says Mum (I bet she's just remembered my age), "is that it starts quite soon, and afterwards I'll have to get back, so it's the film or make-up. What do you say?"

"*Film*," I say quickly. "Um, film, yeah, let's see the film."

In your *face*, Olivia! And I can casually drop it into conversation with Mark too (not that I care). I'm going to be so cool!

"Great!" smiles Mum. "I'll go get the – oh, hang on, I have to take this." She disappears, answering her phone again.

I immediately start picturing my new cool life, where I get to dress impeccably, see amazing films and then report back to my peers about them...

"*Don Ella*, what happens in *Dead Witches*?" (Everyone will have to call me *Don Ella* – like in the five minutes I saw of the *The Godfather* before Dad turned it off.)

"OK, I'll tell you." I'll grin wisely. "But only if you think you can *handle* it." And they'll gasp in fear, and then—

"Ella, Ella?" Mum interrupts my fantasy.

"Where do you want to sit?" I ask her brightly.

"I'm so sorry, darling, I have to go," says Mum. "We'll have to go to the cinema and finish shopping another time."

WHAT? But then how will I make people hang

on my every word as I make pronouncements about *earning respect*?

"Will you be OK getting back to the bus stop with all these bags without me to help you?" she asks.

"Um," I say doubtfully.

"You're going to have to be," says Mum. "I'm really sorry." She gives me a quick awkward chair hug, kisses me on the forehead, and runs.

Hmmmm... Well, I expect everyone will still admire my bracelets.

I soon discover I can't get to the bus stop by myself. It takes me almost five minutes to get out of the diner, and I have to stop twice. This is definitely too many bags. Plus my (admittedly very heavy) normal bag.

I call Jas as soon as I half drag everything to the cinema listings and luckily she is free to come and help me get them all back to my house.

Honestly, thank goodness for Jas. Best, best friend *ever*. I take back any and every mean thing I ever thought about her.

Then, at my house, we have an impromptu fashion show and she admires all of my new purchases. I've never had Jas (or anyone) impressed with my clothes before. It's a great feeling.

We decide to have a mini sleepover in my room, which is so much fun. Dad even agrees to let us order a pizza. He goes a bit tight-lipped over all the things Mum has bought me, but he doesn't say anything. And he STILL hasn't noticed my *Jay-Shees*!

After carrying such heavy things, I am inspired to streamline my bag, as per my mum's advice. I probably don't need nail scissors or this giant hairbrush, I realise. Instead I put in a tiny comb I got from a Christmas cracker.

Jas helps me while we wait for the pizza. And she helps me choose one of my new outfits ready to wear to swimming tomorrow morning. (I can't believe I have trouble *choosing* an outfit.) *Me*. That has literally never happened before. Partly because I sort of only really had two outfits.

This is amazing. I am officially fashionable.*

* May not be that fashionable.

CHAPTER THIRTEEN

Everyone agrees I am very fashionable on Monday morning at school. Well, all three of my friends do. Well, they don't exactly phrase it like that.

"*Someone's* got a spring in their step this morning," Debbie comments as I swan into our form room and sit down at our desks.

"Who, me?" I flutter my eyelashes at her.

"Weirdo," says Debbie, and takes a bite of her Kit Kat.

I chuckle.

"Oooh, I like your bracelets," says Kaya, noticing my wrist.

"Oh, thanks, they're new." I beam, shaking them.

"Careful, Ella, we're not supposed to wear bracelets at school, remember?" says Jas. Why does she have to be such a killjoy? Loads of people wear jewellery to school.

"Oh, don't worry, I'll keep them hidden under my jumper sleeve when any teachers are around," I tell her.

And honestly, I would have totally been able to make Jas *eat* her kind words of concern and friendship if Mrs Allison hadn't made Jas, Tim and me sit with Olivia, Sasha and Grace for PSHCE again.

"Oh, look out, *incoming*," says Olivia, as we miserably approach their clump of desks. (I mean, surely it's someone else's turn to sit with them by now?)

"I keep forgetting Lurch from *The Addams Family* goes to our school," quips Olivia, looking right at me, as we sit down. Grace and Sasha giggle.

I'm so sick of this. I wanted to be *Don Ella*.

"*Lurch* from *The Addams Family*? Bit of a *dated* reference, isn't it, Olivia?" I manage a smirk. "1991 called, it wants its *burns* back." If I can't be *Don Ella*, I can at least be Chandler from *Friends*.

There is a shocked pause, then everyone within earshot laughs. BUTTS look round, chuckling (Mark heard!). Tim guffaws. Even Jas splutters surprised laughter through her fingers. Sasha and Grace do a muted *tut*, like they can't believe I just said that.

Olivia looks momentarily stunned. "It's on Netflix *actually*," she replies tersely, looking indignant.

Ha. (I'm calling that one–nil to me.)

Mrs Allison unknowingly breaks the tension by placing a giant piece of paper on our desks, then carries on meandering round the room, giving out big paper.

Olivia recovers from her shock, then laughs patronisingly. "*Oh dear*. You know what? I'm feeling charitable. I'm going to let you off. I don't think you *really* want to do this with me today."

"Hey, she's got the same bracelets as you," Sasha suddenly observes.

"*What?*" Olivia stares, livid, at my wrists.

"Oh yeah," confirms Grace.

Olivia dramatically facepalms, then says, "OK, you're going to have to take those off."

"No," I say.

"In all seriousness, *I* can't be seen wearing the same bracelets as *you*," explains Olivia.

"That sounds like a whole load of *not my problem*,"

I reply sassily. Sure, I'm recycling old material, but if it ain't broke.

Nearby people are still straining to listen to us, amused. Sasha's and Grace's heads swivel between us.

Olivia tries to pretend she finds all this funny, and shakes her head, like she is dealing with a three-year-old who is insisting they can fly.

"Do you remember when you said 'don't do whatever Ella's doing' fashion-wise?" asks Grace.

"Yes, *thanks*," replies Olivia. Then to me, brightly and patronisingly, she adds, "You can see the bind I'm in."

"Yes. How sad for you," I reply sarcastically.

Mark and Gemma chuckle; other people are tittering.

Olivia starts going red. "Look. It's *really tragic* that you're copying me," she says aggressively, starting to lose her cool. "Everyone is really embarrassed for you. But maybe you should quit while you're *not ahead* and do as I say. You don't want to make an enemy of me."

"Ha!" I laugh. "But we're *such good* friends."

"This is your last chance," she threatens.

"*Whatever*," I reply sarcastically. "Bring it on."

"Right, if I could have your attention now please," Mrs Allison calls to the class. "You should all have a big piece of paper on your desks…"

Everyone's heads reluctantly turn to the front.

"Are you *sure* you're OK?" Jas is still saying, as we walk back from the canteen after lunch. "It's just not like you."

"Jas, isn't it good that I'm sticking up for myself?" I reply patiently.

I'm starting to feel a little bit annoyed with Jas to be honest. I was quite exhilarated after PSHCE, but Jas keeps being all "what have you done?" and taking the shine off it. Now I'm starting to slightly fear potential repercussions. And I hate feeling afraid. Especially after feeling brave for at least ten minutes. It's such a comedown.

"There's sticking up for yourself, and then there's looking for trouble," says Jas dubiously.

Wahwahwah. Classic Jas. Everyone knows bad things only happen if you worry about them too much.

"Ella Hudson!" Miss Gaskew has been waiting

outside the staffroom corridor, apparently ready to pounce.

"Yes ... Miss?"

"Come with me please. I'd like to have a word with you in my office."

Say whaaat now? I look sadly at Jas, who tries not to make her face say *I told you so*, and then I glumly follow Miss Gaskew down the corridor to her office. Stupid Jas being right again. This is all *her* fault.

CHAPTER FOURTEEN

"Wait here a moment," Miss Gaskew tells me as we reach her office door. She goes inside and closes it. Now what? I feel nervous and full of adrenaline.

I wait awkwardly outside and make sure my bracelets are carefully hidden under my jumper sleeve. I wonder if I have time to take them off, just in case? It's a risk. How long will she make me wait here?

"Enter," booms Miss Gaskew.

I step inside the room. "Hello, er, Miss. You … wanted to see me?"

Maybe it's not bad? Maybe she wants to commend me for something…? "Hey, Ella, great job on not wearing trainers for five minutes." "Congratulations on coming fifth from last in the cross-country." "Well

done on eating some salad the other day without even being told to." OK, seems unlikely.

"Ella, thank you. Yes. Come in, shut the door, sit down." I obey.

Miss Gaskew finishes writing something on her desk (like she's too busy for me to be here, even though this was *her* idea) and then looks up at me. "It's come to my attention that you are wearing jewellery to school that is not allowed," says Miss Gaskew.

Ohhhh man. Well played, Olivia, I guess. What an absolute *cow*.

"Did this come to your attention via Olivia by any chance?" I say, hoping I sound unbothered and brave, and that I'm not red or looking intimidated.

"It doesn't matter where it came from, is it true?"

"Ummmm…" I am so busted.

"Could you roll up your jumper sleeves please?" prompts Miss Gaskew.

"Actually I'm a bit cold," I protest lamely.

"NOW."

I roll my innocent sleeve up. "See?"

"Yes, and the other one."

I roll my guilty sleeve up slowly and carefully, but

III

of course the bracelets slip out and jangle together round my wrist.

"Right," says Miss Gaskew, apparently satisfied. "Well, first of all, you can take those off and hand them over to me. You'll get them back at the end of term."

"*WHAT?*" I didn't quite mean to yell that.

"You heard me correctly."

"But that's *ages* away. These are *new*. Can't I just have them back at the end of the day or week? *Please, Miss*." I'm suddenly really worried I might cry.

"Off. Now." Miss Gaskew has prepared an envelope with my name on, which she holds out and shakes, to indicate where I have to put my precious new bracelets.

I *really* hope I don't cry. I start miserably taking them off.

"My mum got me these," I say.

"Well, perhaps your mum needs a refresher on the school uniform guide," says Miss Gaskew, unmoved. My beautiful new bracelets, which make me feel dressed up and special and confident, are now in a horrible brown school envelope.

Miss Gaskew folds it shut. "You know Olivia has

these exact bracelets," I tell Miss Gaskew. "Why has she got away with it? She's played you."

"Olivia is a model student, and she's concerned about you," reveals Miss Gaskew.

Model student? Not in PSHCE. I *knew* it was her that had told on me.

"What? Olivia *hates* me," I reply dismissively. "She literally doesn't want me to wear the same bracelets as her because I'm not cool enough."

"It sounds like you might be having self-esteem issues," says Miss Gaskew. "Ella, rest assured you don't need to worry about things like being *cool enough*."

"Ha!" This is infuriating. "Try telling Olivia, though."

"Ella, is everything all right at home?"

"Yeah, why?" I ask.

"You've generally always been a very well-behaved, fairly conformist student, but in the last weeks you've taken to flouting school uniform rules and causing public scenes. First the shoes, now these bracelets. You recently pretended to faint when I was talking to you, and Olivia said you had what she described as a 'meltdown' –" Miss Gaskew does air quotes – "when she told you to take off your bracelets earlier this morning."

I sigh, frustrated. "Oh my *god*."

"Language please."

"Miss Gaskew, there was a wasp and I tripped over when I was talking to you that time. Olivia is *lying*. I didn't have a meltdown this morning. If anything, *she* did!"

"You sound angry."

"Well, I suppose I am."

"Then it seems plausible to me that you might have had a meltdown."

"I *definitely* didn't." I try to sound as calm as possible.

"Ella, lots of teenagers go through stages where they feel angry and have low self-esteem. Unfortunately it's all part of growing up. I want to let you know we're here if you ever need to talk about anything."

"But you're not listening to me."

"Well, I think I've made myself perfectly clear."

"I don't think I've made *my*self perfectly clear," I say.

"What would you like to add?" asks Miss Gaskew.

"Olivia hates me," I say.

"I think this might be projection," says Miss Gaskew.

Honestly. Did she swallow a psychology book for *idiots*?

"Olivia is a liar who is trying to get me in trouble," I attempt.

"I'm not interested in tittle-tattle," says Miss Gaskew.

"Except when Olivia is doing it," I retort.

"OK. Ella, this is getting us nowhere. I've offered you an olive branch but if you don't want to accept it, that's fine."

I *hate* the power games that teachers try to play. Like, get over yourselves already. And, P.S., your olive branch is a twig covered in excrement.

"Fine," I say.

"So, let's move on to your punishment."

"WHAT?" I yell. "Stealing my stuff isn't my punishment?"

"Confiscating your stuff, in line with our school rules," Miss Gaskew corrects. "It's probably wise not to call your teachers thieves, Ella."

She stares at me expectantly. Oh my *god*, I think

she's waiting for an apology. "Umm... Sorry?" I offer.

"Thank you. Right. It's another lunchtime detention I'm afraid, and I'm going to be contacting your dad. Just because this is so close to your last infraction. You may go."

I *hate* Olivia.

What the actual *hell* is going on with the world?

CHAPTER FIFTEEN

The bell goes for Year Eight lunch and the rest of my form stampedes out. *Stupid detention.* I'm alone for a moment. *Stupid Olivia.* Wait, I'm alone. *Hmmm.* I quickly go over to the bag that she's left on her desk. God, I hate Olivia and her horrible gloaty smug face. I quickly take out my Tippex and write "UGLY COW" on her bag. I figure this is the insult that will hurt her the *most*. Ha!

"Hey." Mark has re-entered the form room.

"Nothing!" I blurt guiltily and drop Olivia's bag.

"I forgot my pen," he says, coming over. His desk is near Olivia's, hence how he managed to hear most of our exchanges. I feel really hot as he approaches. "I've got detention," he says.

"Me too," I reply.

He leans over and spies my handiwork on Olivia's bag. He smells of mint and boy deodorant.

"Nice," he comments.

"I don't know what you mean," I reply.

"Sure." He nods. His hair flops in his eyes momentarily. He smiles. "Your secret's safe with me. She had it coming."

We start walking out of the form together, towards our allotted detention classroom. "You did the can machine too, didn't you?" he asks quietly.

"No. Ha! *What?* I don't know what you mean," I say stupidly.

He chuckles. "I'm not going to tell on you. I'm not *Olivia*."

"I still don't know what you mean," I insist pointlessly.

I worry I'm going red. Maybe I *should* admit it to him? It might be nice to share a secret with Mark… (For completely normal reasons, obviously.)

"Fine. But if I ever meet the *Tippex Bandit*, I'd like to tell them I like their style," says Mark.

OMG that is the coolest nickname I have ever been given! *Tippex Bandit*… The me of three weeks ago who kept getting called "povvo shoes" and "Miss

Goody Two Shoes gomer" would never believe it.

"OK, OK," I grin gleefully. "It *was* me. But you can't tell anyone."

Mark looks at me, smiling, and we lock eyes briefly. "Cool," he says simply. A shoot of excitement rises inside me.

Mark said I am cool. Take that three-weeks-ago me! I'm basically *Don Ella* already.

"What did you get detention for?" I ask him.

"Oh. I *think* it was because I threw a ball at Mr Brown's head, but he *says* it was for not listening to instructions properly or whatever."

I chuckle, emboldened by my new coolness. "His instructions are so *boring*," I joke along. "What does he *expect*?"

"*Exactly*." Mark chuckles too. (I am cool *and* funny.)

We're nearly at the allotted classroom, which is a science lab, because Mr Brown teaches science as well as PE. "It'll probably be lines," says Mark. We pause outside the door and lock eyes again. Is it me, or does something pass between us? "Well, see you on the other side." He goes into the room.

Damn, I totally forgot to look at which way his feet

were pointing like that body language library book said to do. OK, mental note: try to look at Mark's feet, then I'll know for sure if he fancies me.

Mr Brown tells me to sit on the front bench, next to Mark. I guess he thinks we don't know each other and we won't talk.

I have to write, "I must not wear jewellery to school," fifty times on a piece of lined paper I am given. Mark has to write, "I must listen properly to instructions."

"You will work in silence," instructs Mr Brown. Then he sits at his desk at the front and starts reading a newspaper.

"I feel like Bart Simpson," I whisper to Mark.

Mark chuckles. "First lunchtime detention? The novelty soon wears off."

"Do you think Mr Brown would notice if I just wrote the first and last few lines and scribbled the rest?" I whisper.

"Yes," Mark replies. "Me and Liam did that once. We both had to write a hundred more lines."

"*Daaaamn,*" I whisper in a funny voice. "There must be a way to Derren Brown him."

Mark looks at me and laughs again. "You're

120

suddenly getting a lot of detentions," he whispers. "Coming over to the dark side?"

"*Two?*" I try to sound scornful. "You sound like my dad. Except he didn't say *dark side*; I don't think he's ever seen a *Star Wars* film."

"That's weird," whispers Mark. "Normally old people love *Star Wars*."

"I know, *right?*" I whisper. "It's like he's a traitor to his generation or something."

We both laugh quietly. I can't believe how easy it is to talk to Mark. Well, *whisper*. I realise I'm having *fun* in detention. That can't be right.

I think Mark is having fun too because eventually he suggests that we should swap numbers.

"*What?*" I whisper, not entirely able to hide my surprise, and hopefully not looking *too* keen. I can't see his feet; they're under the desk.

"Yeah," whispers Mark. "And we should hang out. Like at the weekend. If you're ever around?"

"You want to hang out?" (Oh my god, he totally does fancy me!)

"Yeah. Come out with us. If you like."

Us. All of BUTTS. (OK, he might not fancy me.) But he *might*. What on earth would it be like to hang out with BUTTS? "Uh, yeah, maybe," I whisper.

But seriously. What the actual *hell* is going on with the world?

CHAPTER
SIXTEEN

"Right!" shouts Mrs Williams on Thursday. I pull out my maths books and thump them on to my desk. I'm still sitting next to Gemma. "Settle down. Settle down, please. We shall be continuing our work on Pythagoras' theorem." Everyone groans.

I underline the date at the top of a new page in my maths book, and Gemma looks over at it and laughs. "What?" I whisper.

"Your title. You're calling this lesson '*More Triangles*'?"

"Yes," I agree, nonplussed.

"Here, look." Gemma finishes underlining something. I look over and she has entitled her new page "More Bloody Triangles".

I burst out laughing unexpectedly and have to

cover my mouth with my hands, suddenly seeing what she was getting at.

"Everything all right, Gemma and Ella?" queries Mrs Williams suspiciously.

"Top-notch, Miss," replies Gemma. "Can't get enough of these triangles!"

I force myself to stop laughing.

"Good." Mrs Williams frowns, and goes back to addressing the class.

I scribble something in my rough book. "Oi, Gemma," I whisper, pointing, "this is what I'm going to title my next maths lesson."

Gemma looks over to where I've written and underlined "Seriously? Triangles AGAIN??"

Gemma guffaws really loudly, and Mrs Williams has to stop the lesson again. "Gemma!" she shouts. "What is going *on* over there?"

"Sorry, Miss!" Gemma straightens her face and forces herself to stop giggling.

"I do not want to hear another *peep* out of you for the rest of the lesson. Do you hear me?" barks Mrs Williams.

"Yes, sorry," says Gemma.

Mrs Williams goes back to droning and pointing

at the whiteboard.

There's a pause. I whisper to Gemma, "Peep." She bites her hand to stop herself from laughing. I grin. I can't believe I'm having so much fun with a BUTTS.

"I never knew you were funny," Gemma whispers to me. "I thought you were a *goody-goody*. You and Jasmine and those other two."

"Oh no, Jas is really funny too," I whisper back.

Gemma pulls a face, like she doesn't believe for a second that Jas could be amusing.

"No," I argue, still whispering. "We're just *secretly* funny because we're shy. Jas is hilarious."

"Believe it when I see it," whispers Gemma dubiously. "She doesn't seem funny; she seems pretty judgemental."

"No," I whisper. "You're wrong." Though actually, I realise I have felt a little judged by Jas lately. But overall she's been really supportive and nice about my mum and everything. "You should talk to her," I whisper. "You'll see."

"If you say so." Gemma starts scribbling on her rough book. Then passes it to me.

She's drawn a cartoon triangle pointing a gun at its own head, with a speech bubble saying, "Even *I* can't take much more of this!"

I can't help it; I laugh out loud before I can stop myself. I clasp both hands over my mouth, but it's too late.

"THAT'S IT!" Mrs Williams shouts from the front. "Gemma Fitzgerald! You are clearly corrupting Ella Hudson! I can see I'm going to have to move you again."

"No!" I hear myself yell. The whole class is staring at us.

I don't fully know what I'm doing, I just know that it's not fair for Gemma to get the sole blame when we were both messing about, just because she's got the bad reputation.

"No?" Mrs Williams sounds incredulous.

"She's not corrupting me," I hear myself reply. "That was *my* fault, Miss. I accidentally made a mistake. Gemma was … helping me."

"I see." Mrs Williams knows this is a lie, but clearly isn't quite sure what to do about it. "If either of you make any more noise for the rest of the lesson, you can both join me for lunchtime detention today. Understand?"

We both nod mutely.

"I can't believe you stuck up for me," says Gemma, packing up her books at the end of the lesson, once we are finally allowed to talk.

"Oh," I say. "Well, it was my fault really."

"Still," says Gemma.

"Um, can we talk?" Jas arrives at our maths desks.

"Oh, hi, Jas," I say amicably. "I was just telling Gemma how funny—"

"Yeah, great," Jas interrupts and shoots a suspicious look at Gemma. "Now?" she prompts me.

"Yes," I reply, scrabbling my books together.

"You don't seem funny," Gemma tells Jas. "Say something funny."

"*What*?" Jas looks cross. "I'm not *auditioning* for your maths comedy show," she replies snidely.

"I don't get it," replies Gemma with a smirk.

"Now?" Jas repeats to me.

I nod. I don't have time to explain the context to everyone.

"Uh, I have to go," I say to Gemma.

"Fine. We'll come and find you at lunch," Gemma calls after me, as Jas practically drags me out of the room.

Lunch starts off quite awkwardly with Jas. Then it gets a tiny bit better. Then it gets worse.

"What the hell is going on?" Jas queries.

It's not like her to be this riled up. She's usually the calm one.

"What?" I ask her. We sit opposite each other in the canteen, each holding our sandwiches.

"We could have moved back next to each other," says Jas.

Ohhhh. Yeah. Of course! Whoops. "Oh," I manage. How on earth did I forget that?

"You've been complaining about it non-stop for the last two weeks. What's changed? Why do you suddenly prefer to sit next to Gemma from BUTTS than *me*?"

Oh no. I've done a bad thing. Oh man, I so didn't mean to hurt Jas's feelings. How on earth can I explain this?

"It's the justice, Jas," I attempt.

"*Justice?*" Jas is not impressed with this answer.

"Look, Gemma and I were both messing about, and just because of her reputation she was getting the blame. And that's not fair."

"Why were you messing about in maths?" asks Jas.

It was fun. "I was bored," I reply. "I'm really sorry, Jas," I say. "I wasn't thinking. I reacted in the moment. I would actually much rather sit next to you." Almost definitely. *No*, definitely.

"OK." Jas sounds a bit mollified. We eat some of our sandwiches.

"Actually, Jas," I say, "you'd be surprised. BUTTS are much nicer than we thought. I had detention with some of them the other day as well. And they're actually OK. They're really funny. Mark is, um… But maybe you'd like them if we all hung out together?"

"Hey! There she is!" Gemma booms loudly behind me. Then suddenly Mark, Liam and Gemma are sitting next to Jas and me, all squeezed on to our table.

"Oh, goody, here's my chance," says Jas sarcastically, looking uncomfortable.

"They finally cleaned 'TAX-AVOIDING SCUM' off the can machine," announces Liam.

Gemma says "shame" at the same time as Jas says "good". OK. I probably won't tell Jas it was me. Mark winks at me conspiratorially. He actually winks! I don't think I've ever been winked at by a boy before. I glow secretly, and look down smiling. Still can't see his feet.

"Anyone started Mrs Snider's history homework yet?" asks Liam.

"Is that the one where we have to write about who we'd pick, if we could meet any historical figure to have a conversation with?" I ask, trying to look normal.

"I have," says Jas. "Marco Polo."

"No, it has to be a real person," says Liam, while Gemma laughs.

Jas shoots me this look that says *You really want to hang out with these idiots?*

"Marco Polo *was* a real person," she says.

"Ha! No, it's that game!" laughs Gemma.

Jas shoots me another look that says *Feel free to correct them any time.* Everyone does weirdly look at me then. How come I'm the arbitrator?

"Actually," I say, "Marco Polo *was* a real person. He was a merchant trader who travelled from Venice to China. But lots of things *are* named after him. So, you know, sort of everyone is right."

"Cool," says Jas, rolling her eyes. "Well, I've

finished my lunch, so…" She gets up.

I get up too. "See you guys later!" I call over my shoulder as I scurry after her.

Why does Jas have to be so difficult? Still, Mark winked at me, that was exciting.

CHAPTER SEVENTEEN

"I just don't understand *why* you wore bracelets to school," says Dad, closing a kitchen cupboard.

I scream inwardly. "You know there are people starving in the world, right?" I retort. "Bracelets are *so* not important in the big scheme of things."

"But you knew the rules." Dad sounds genuinely baffled by my behaviour. So baffled that he's still going on about it on *Saturday*.

"Oh, come on, Dad, we're better than this," I attempt pointlessly. "Please let's not have *such* a clichéd father–daughter argument."

"Well, look," says Dad seriously, "it's never too early to start thinking about your future. Try to stop getting detentions. You need a good track record, show you can play by the rules, keep your head down, so you can one day get a good job."

"Oh, whoop-ti-do," I say sarcastically. "That's so inspiring, Dad, thanks. Shouldn't you be telling me to aim for the stars? Or that I can be anything I set my mind to?"

"Oh, I see," says Dad. "I suppose you want to be a *pop star* or something, do you?"

Obviously I *don't* want to be a pop star.

"I could be a pop star!" I yell indignantly.

"Sure," says Dad, looking annoyingly amused.

That's *it*. "I'm forming a band!" I storm out and slam the kitchen door behind me as I stump upstairs.

"I don't like doors slamming!" Dad calls after me.

I text Jas that we immediately need to form a band to teach my dad a lesson, and she sends me back a gif of Michelle Obama facepalming. Which makes me think she *might* not be completely on board.

Sometimes it's annoying that Jas is so much better at the Internet than me. I'll never find a good gif to send back that says "you are a bad friend, thanks for *nothing*". Honestly. Why does no one support my every whim? It's so unfair.

I've *had* it with my dad lately. I'm so bored of his

lectures. I really do want to teach him a lesson. I get out my "make-up bag" that I have cobbled together from discarded bits from Jas and freebies from magazines. I don't really know what I'm doing, but I'm pretty sure I can teach my dad a lesson with this.

"You're not going out like that. People will think you're ill." Dad takes one look at me and puts down the plate he's washing. I almost want to slow-clap his lack of originality.

"It's for my new band," I tell him. "We're going to be punks." Obviously I knew Dad wouldn't understand about *smoky eye*. He doesn't even really like smoky bacon.

"Well, you look like a zombie." Dad obviously wants to cement his new clichéd Dad stereotype.

"Huh. Zombies *wish* they looked like this," I retort.

Not quite sure why I'm *boasting* I look better than a zombie. It should really go without saying. And zombies probably don't wish they looked like me. They just want to eat brains or flesh, depending on which zombie story you ascribe to. Or— But look, the point is, a *lesson* is being taught. Ha.

"Well, whatever. But you're not going out looking

like that." Dad turns back to the sink.

Wait, that's not the lesson. The lesson isn't *me* learning to toe the line; it's *him* learning to let me spread my wings and *back off* with his boring criticisms *or else*. I can't believe I'm *losing* the lesson battle. Nooooo.

"Well, you're only fifty per cent of my parents now that Mum's ... able to see me." (Is that the right way of putting it?) Dad stiffens but carries on washing up. "Why don't I ask *her* permission instead?" I get my phone out of my pocket.

Dad turns back to face me, looking a bit sad. "I *don't* want to spea— get into an argument about this," he says quietly.

"Well, can I just go out then?" I ask. "I'll stay at Mum's this weekend, so you don't have to see my face, since you hate it so much."

Dad turns back to the washing up. "Fine," he mumbles.

Yes! I won! And I can stay at Mum's at the weekend and have *fun*. And have *freedom* and not be lectured all day long. Woohoo! Mum gets it. Mum will understand.

"What have you done to your face?" Mum stares at me in horror, then seems to calm down as she realises it's only make-up. Not quite the *hats off to your rebellious streak, kiddo* I was hoping for.

"It's smoky eye, Mum."

"Ah. Oh," says Mum. "Right…"

I feel like a three-year-old who's given their mum a piece of paper with some scribble on it, and she's had to go, "*Of course* I could see it was a ship. What a good ship!"

"Did you copy a magazine or a … YouTube video?" she asks, dumping my bag on the sofa.

"Um, no. I just kind of made it up as I went along," I admit.

In all honesty, I'd been so keen to make sure both eyes were even, I hadn't quite been sure when to stop. One eye would look wonky, so I'd add more eyeliner, then the other one wouldn't match, so they both kept growing bigger and bigger. Then finally I cleverly thought to smudge the edges to cover up any mistakes.

"Riiight," says Mum, looking at me. "I think it might be time for your first make-up lesson. I'll make us a coffee."

CHAPTER EIGHTEEN

OK. I don't want to get over-excited and "over-idealise" my mum (or whatever Jas was going on about the other day) but, OMG, my mum is *brilliant*. She has taught me to use a wet cotton bud to take off excess eyeliner and neaten the edges. *And* she let me drink coffee.

Maybe Dad is right and I watch too much TV, because these two things combined have immediately made me feel like I must be a high-powered fashion executive working in New York.

"Is *fashion executive* a job?" I ask Mum. And then I go back to making the appropriate *mascara face* (as far as I can tell, tilting your head back and looking down your nose at a mirror).

"I don't know. Probably." Mum smiles and puts

the mascara wand back in the tiny bottle. Well, that's settled. My new career is waiting for me. "All done. Have a look." She holds up the mirror and I gasp.

I look amazing! I mean, I look about *twenty-five*. I reckon I could convincingly buy a lottery ticket or a house like this. Mum's put pale pink lip gloss on my lips and a tiny bit of glitter at the top of my cheeks, but the main difference is my eyes! The eyeliner really defines them. And the mascara kind of makes them pop. I can't stop staring at them in the mirror.

"I love it!" I manage. "Let's take a selfie!"

Mum immediately moves into the perfect pose and helps me angle the phone. It's so great having a parent that:

(a) Knows what a selfie is.

(b) Doesn't go, "Oh, you mean a self-portrait photo" every time you try to take one of you both (even though you have repeatedly told him that's *not* what it's called).

I look at my face in the mirror again. "Dad would never let me wear make-up like this."

"Oh, he will," says Mum dismissively. "He'll be fine. Just doesn't like change." Mum drains her coffee and refills her cup from her cool little coffee jug that sits on a hotplate. "Top-up?"

"No, thanks." I'm kind of buzzing and feel slightly full of nervous energy. "Dad said I was too young and that I was so beautiful I didn't *need* make-up." I feel a small twinge inside me. That's actually a really nice thing to say.

"Well," says Mum. "He's right, you are beautiful and you don't *need* make-up. But you're thirteen now and make-up is *fun*!" She smiles conspiratorially.

Yeah! Make-up is *fun*! And I'm thirteen for crying out loud. Dad has got to learn to move with the times and lighten up. I mean, look at this – me and Mum have seamlessly entered this impressive new phase in our relationship. Mum teaches me how to be a cool teenager, and I'm totally grown-up and forgiving that she left. If *I* can move with the times and get over their divorce so efficiently, the least my dad can do is accept I'm practically an adult now. And I'll show my mum that I don't need everything to be perfect. I'm happy just hanging out with her again.

"Oh my god, Mum, I've had a brilliant idea!" I exclaim suddenly. "Let's do each other's hair next. No, better yet, let's have a sleepover! We can bring our duvets into your living room, and put our pyjamas on, and watch DVDs, and eat popcorn, and gossip. And you can give me loads of *advice* about *life*!"

Mum looks nervous for a second, then laughs. "Well. I'm not sure I'm exactly an *expert* at giving *advice*." She waves a hand dismissively. "And I wouldn't sleep on the floor if I were you, in case of the silverfish." (What are silverfish?) She yawns distractedly. "*Plus* I'm going out tonight."

"Are you?" I'm surprised. "But you knew *I* was coming."

"Yeah, I know, but you only texted me two hours ago. Aren't you going out too? It's Saturday night."

Mum hasn't been gone *that long*. When did I ever go out on Saturday night? (Unless she's counting going to Jas's house?) Or maybe now I look so grown up with this make-up on she's mistaken me for someone with a mega social life?

"Yeah," I say carefully. "Um. Yeah, I often … if not always, go out and do … *cool stuff* on Saturday nights." (Why exactly am I lying to my own mother about who I am?)

Mum smiles. "That's good."

"Um. But you know what?" I cast around. "I'm … um … happy to cancel my plans just this once. Why don't we stay in? Why don't we stay in and have a nice catch-up? I'm a bit tired anyway."

"Oh, well, I'd love to, but I can't just cancel my plans," says Mum.

"Sure you can. I just did," I lie. I just totally cancelled my invisible, non-existent plans.

"I'm really sorry, sweetheart. I can't get out of it now. Next time."

"*Please*," I say.

Mum looks genuinely pained for a moment. "Look, I really, *really* would if I could, but I can't. Not this time. I *promise* we'll do something fun next time."

"But … um," I say in a small voice, "I thought we were going to … you know, you said you wanted to see me again, and … everything."

"Of *course* I do!" says Mum earnestly. "I want to spend as much time with you as possible. I just didn't realise you thought that meant tonight."

"OK," I say sadly.

Mum grins, looking faintly amused, and tries to inject some levity into her voice. "We're not joined at the hip, Ella!" she chuckles, then suddenly starts to look more serious. "I still have a social life. I'm not just *someone's mum*." (Not *someone* – me.) "I have a business to run now. I need more notice for some things. It's not my fault."

"I said OK," I repeat.

I mean, I don't want to overact or anything, but this is definitely the most unfair thing to happen to anyone ever. Wait, hang on –

"Am I going to be here on my ... own?" I ask.

"Well, yes. Or you can do your going-out plans. Whatever you like."

"How?" I ask.

"Well ... buses." Mum looks a little perplexed. "You know about buses. I saw you get off one."

"You'll let me get the bus?" I almost whisper. "At ... *night-time?*" I don't know if I'm more in awe or terrified.

Mum's phone pings and she looks at it and starts typing. "Of course," says Mum. I *think* at me. "I mean, be back in time for your curfew or whatever. What does your dad say? Eight? Nine? Surely not ten?"

No, not ten, I think. *Because Dad won't even let me go to the cinema with friends in the safety of a car!* Mum just assumes I have some grown-up curfew situation. This is incredible. (I thought they were in contact with each other? They must just be doing minimum stuff, not really getting into anything.)

"*Hmmm. Where's my...?*" Mum mumbles to herself, tapping her phone.

"Ha! *Ten!*" I laugh.

Mum looks up from her phone, still distracted. "OK then, ten." She *appears* to be addressing me. Is she *joking*?

"Ten?" I query.

Mum's phone starts ringing. She ignores it and looks back at me. "Oh yes, go for it. Have fun!" She glances back down and presses ignore on her phone.

"What?" I say.

"What?" says Mum. "Where were we? Oh yes! Great. It's settled then. We can both have a fun night out and dish the dirt and gossip in the morning over coffee. Like in that sitcom."

I struggle to think of a sitcom where a mother and daughter discuss their nights out over coffee. "*Absolutely Fabulous*?" I venture, unsure.

"No, no, silly. We'll be like what's-their-names. Monica and Rachel."

"Like *Friends*?"

"Best friends," smiles Mum. "Like roommates." She looks at her watch, drains her coffee and stands up. "Oh, and if you end up crashing at a friend's house, text me so I don't worry."

"Um. OK," I say.

"Oh, and if you wear your new jacket," says Mum, "don't wear that jumper underneath; it looks better without."

"OK," I say. Mum knows what she's talking about.

"I'll give you my spare key," says Mum. Oh my god, this is so cool! *Finally,* I'm a latch-key kid. "I just need to call back— Actually I'd better give you a quick tour of the place," adds Mum. "And some money."

"Great!" I reply.

Mum hands me a tenner. "Is that enough? It's just emergency money."

"Yeah, thanks!"

Mum starts the tour. "So, this place is a work in progress, obviously. But at least I've got the fridge." She gestures across at the open-plan kitchen, where the biggest and most amazing fridge I've ever seen stands prominently, dwarfing the rest of the shabby and ramshackle stuff. It doesn't really fit in.

"It's an amazing fridge," I comment. It has an ice machine, and water, and buttons that make it look more like a computer.

Mum nods. "It makes the tea and sings a song and everything. Only the best, you know me."

I nod uncertainly as she leads me to the bathroom. "There's no door handle at the moment, but on the plus side that means you can't lock yourself in!" explains Mum, heading off to the next room.

"This is my bedroom. I'm going to change all this. And fix that window. It's going to look amazing when it's finished."

"Brilliant!" I force a smile. I know I said it doesn't have to be *perfect*, but I sort of liked it better before Mum gave me the tour and I had to pay attention to how crummy and dilapidated her flat is.

〜〜〜〜↘

Never mind that now. I've got to take this face out and show it off to people. I've pragmatically decided to forgive Jas for her sarcastic gif earlier. She's bound to want a sleepover, and popcorn. I really would like some popcorn now.

I text Jas:

> M8! U have got 2 C my new face. Mum did my make-up. Wanna have a sleepover at urs 2nite?
> I can teach you my nu skillz.

A moment later I get back:

> Photo me *winky smiley (tongue out) face*

My phone keeps pinging with her other replies. When she's not sending well-chosen gifs, Jas always seems to send stream-of-consciousness messages. I WhatsApp her the selfie my mum and I took earlier, then read her other missives:

> Wld love 2 but can't 2nite. Got family round.

> Am having my cheeks pinched and told 2 eat more. LOL.

> OMG, pic is amazing! *dancing women, hands clapping*

I try not to feel too dejected later as I hunt through Mum's kitchen for food. These days, Mum appears just to live off coffee, rice cakes and cottage cheese. None of which appeal to me. Luckily I find a stash of microwave chips in the state-of-the-art freezer.

As I sit at Mum's small, wobbly, make-up strewn kitchen table, eating the metallic-tasting slimy chips,

I try not to feel too jealous of Jas eating delicious home-cooked food. She'll be fussed over and appreciated by her loving family. While I've got one parent in a huff, and the other one gone AWOL again. Compared with Jas, I've been very unlucky with my parents, I think.

No. I refuse to feel sorry for myself. I should go out and take advantage of my new freedom. OMG, *I should text Mark!* Should I? *Hmmmm.*

To see how it looks, I type out:

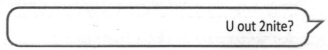

U out 2nite?

I'm about to delete it and try a more jokey version, when Jas sends me a picture of her dinner and I accidentally press send on the text. Well, that's that then.

I continue to eat chips, trying not to feel anxious.

Maybe he's busy. Or his phone's off. Or he's having a night in but is too embarrassed to say?

My phone pings. Yes! I'm going OUT on a Saturday night! I am a Party Animal!*

* May not be a Party Animal.

CHAPTER NINETEEN

I feel a twinge of guilty nervousness on the bus to town, but I manage to force it to one side. I *deserve* to have some *fun* for once. Dad and Jas have been really critical of me this week. It will be good to hang out with people who are laid-back and don't nag me all the time. This is going to be *exciting*!

This is so *not* exciting.

I can't believe I yearned for so long to see how the other half live (the other half being the people who are allowed out at night-time). I imagined it was the height of cool, freedom and rebellion. What a let-down.

This? This is what I've been missing out on? Freezing on street corners, drinking cans of Coke, complaining about school. I can drink Coke at Jas's house. (Dad refuses to buy it for some reason.) And it's *warm* there. (The house, not the Coke.)

In fact, I can do *all* of this at Jas's house, with the only difference being that sometimes if we complain about school *too* much, Jas's dad might overhear and tell us we are very lucky to have such a good education. And then Jas looks embarrassed when he's gone and says, "He just doesn't *get it*, because in India they treat teachers like gods or whatever. And he's just forgotten how annoying algebra really is."

I shiver and pull my jacket tighter round me. Why did I let my mum talk me out of wearing my jumper? What kind of parent tells you *not* to wear a jumper? Dad is *obsessed* with jumpers. Then again, he also thinks things look like vests when they're clearly not vests. So I don't know what to believe.

I mean, I suppose it was *almost* fun to start with because Gemma seemed impressed with my make-up. Well, she said something that sounded like the word "peng", which I will Google later. But it *sounded* positive. But now I'm bored. I'm disappointingly bored. Everyone is *still* talking about Mrs Miller.

OK, Mrs Miller is a bit annoying. And OK, *sure*, it *was* really weird when she wore that eyepatch for a week and just didn't even reference it. But I'm ninety per cent sure it *wasn't* because she had pirate-itus or a black eye. I think it was something to do with her glasses prescription.

"She started a pub fight, definitely," Liam states confidentially.

The others giggle.

"No, no, she has an X-Men power," retorts Gemma. "Like Cyclops."

"But that would be both eyes," says Mark.

"Doesn't have to be," defends Gemma.

Aagghh. I'm cold and hungry and increasingly annoyed. Hang on. I've still got the ten pounds my mum gave me before we left. Maybe I should cut my losses, buy a spicy chicken burger, and get the bus home back to Mum's. *Oooh*. Yes. That sounds really good actually.

I mean, *I think* my mum meant it was emergency money, as in, if I needed a taxi, but food is *technically* an emergency if she's not going to provide me with a proper meal.

"I'm going to take off," I tell them.

"Tight curfew? Got to get home to *Daddy*?" smirks Liam.

"No," I answer. "I'm staying at my mum's tonight anyway. And she doesn't care what time I get back." I realise this is true as I say it. Oh. Is it? I mean, she does *care*. She said ten; she's just … busy.

"So you *can* stay out then?" Mark smiles at me hopefully.

"Well, yeah." I realise I have snookered myself into staying cold and bored for longer. "For a *bit*." Dagnammit. "What's the plan, though?" I ask them.

They all stare at me incredulously, then look at each other.

"The *plan*?" repeats Gemma.

"Yeah, I mean, are we going to do something fun, or…?"

They look at each other again. "We can have fun," says Mark, flashing his cheeky grin.

"Yeah, we can *have fun*," echoes Liam, but somehow more ominously. "How much money have you got on you?" he asks me.

"Just ten pounds," I say.

"That's fine," says Liam. (Did he just exchange an extra smirk with Gemma?) "That's how much it costs." He reaches out his hand as if he's expecting me to give him my tenner.

"How much *what* costs?" I ask, taking a step back.

"The spray paint."

So it turns out ten pounds can buy three cans of spray paint and a load of sweets for everyone from our town's weird Poundland-esque seven-eleven.

I'm kind of really annoyed with myself for letting them take *all* of my money and spending it on crap I didn't want. But also, I'm kind of intrigued as to what will happen now. It'd better be good. I really wanted that chicken burger.

"You're all right, you are, Ella," Gemma tells me, chewing her fizzy wand as we all walk along the street towards the bridge.

So there's that. That's nice. I guess.

Still, mental note: *never* answer the question "How much money have you got?" truthfully, especially if you are intimidated by the asker and the amount is more than you want to lose. I've learnt my lesson. I can feel myself becoming more street savvy already.

"Right. This is the place," Liam announces, peering around as we head into the underpass. It looks like a skate park crossed with a wasteland. All concrete and litter with the occasional weed poking through.

Everything is covered in graffiti – the walls, the arch, the structure of the bridge. It looks like a film set, if you were going to film a scene about murder. Or graffiti.

"What have we come here for?" I ask them pointlessly. (I am fairly confident they aren't murderers.)

"To tag," answers Liam.

OMG, they're *all* tagging! I keep looking round, back the way we came, but there's no one else about. We're safe to break the law. Is this illegal? It must be.

Gemma and Mark are mainly writing swear words or drawing ... well, let's call it anatomy. Liam is doing odd squiggles that he claims are his own personal tag.

I watch them, nervous but fascinated. They are so bad! They don't care. Imagine being that free. I am not that free.

"Hey, your go." Mark stops and offers me the can he's holding.

"Um…" I stammer, unsure.

"She not done it yet?" Gemma calls over her shoulder, then goes back to what she's doing. "Thought you wanted to have *fun*?"

"I thought you'd be all over this," says Mark, "especially after the can machine."

That was a secret! Mark told my secret.

Everyone stops and looks at me. "Was that *you*?" marvels Liam.

"Nice," concedes Gemma. "School property and everything."

"Now you *have* to do it!" Liam comes over, proffering his can.

"It's easy." Gemma joins them. She starts giving me a demonstration. "Shake it. Hold it about that far—"

"Sshh," Mark interrupts.

Everyone freezes, and we hear the noise of footsteps and male voices walking along the road towards us.

"It's the police!" shouts Liam. "This way!"

We all leg it towards the country path that will lead us back towards town the long way round.

"Hey!" calls a male voice.

"Run!" squeals Gemma.

We run and run as fast as we can. We don't even stop until we're all the way back in town, and round the side of the fish and chip shop. Then we lean against the alley wall, panting.

This is genuinely the most exhilarating and exciting thing that's ever happened to me. My heart is beating so hard in my chest and I feel *alive*. I can't help but grin at the others. I'm an *outlaw* now!

Liam peers round the wall, looks both ways, then comes back. "Looks all clear," he states. "But we should go our separate ways just in case." We nod. "Remember to keep your hands in your pockets in well-lit areas."

"You can go first if you like, Ella," says Mark.

I nod and head off into the night, a new person. I feel like I could do or be *anything*. Nothing can fence me in. I smile as I walk. I'm *free.**

* May not be completely free.

CHAPTER TWENTY

OK. I will admit some of my euphoria does fade by the time I'm getting into bed at Mum's flat and the worry sets in. I mean, technically I didn't *do* anything wrong. Except ... I did buy the spray paint. That must make me an accomplice? In the eyes of the law? I think I just did aiding and abetting. To a *crime*. A full-on crime. What if there are CCTV cameras? I shudder.

I try not to picture the police storming the flat to arrest me and sit up reading my library book for a bit. But it's about UFOs and I can't really get into it.

Mum still isn't back.

I really should go to sleep I suppose. I decide to leave the lights on (so that Mum can see when she eventually does get back – not because I'm scared of the dark or anything. I am basically a hero) and eventually drift off.

Should I wake my mum? I mean, I'm really hungry. Why doesn't she even have bread in? I could sort myself out if she had bread in. I mean, I've still got to get to swimming. Should I just go? Oh, thank god.

"Good morning." Mum enters the kitchen in her dressing gown, gets herself a pint of water from the tap and switches the coffee machine on. "This place was lit up like Buckingham Palace last night," she comments.

"I'm kind of hungry," I say. "Do you have any bread or Weetabix or anything? I couldn't find any."

"Nah," says Mum. "I'm so busy I mainly eat on the go. Terrible habit really. I'll get a routine once things calm down. But at the moment I eat in so rarely – stuff always goes off."

I should tell her about how Dad always puts a spare loaf of bread in the freezer, so that we don't ever run out, and it doesn't go off. Not sure how to phrase it... *Hey, I'm not telling you how to do your job, but...*

"Great," I reply. "Hey, Mum, guess what, Dad keeps bread in the freezer."

"Yep, that sounds like him," agrees Mum.

My hint is lost in translation. How do I… "Look. I'm really hungry," I blurt out.

"Oh, don't worry, I'll take you out for breakfast," says Mum cheerily. "No freezer bread for you today. Just let me have a shower first."

"OK, but I have to meet Jas for swimming in—"

Mum isn't listening; she's already left the room with her fresh cup of coffee. She didn't actually offer me any. I mean, that's fine. I'll pour myself some. I am a grown-up, after all.

"Wow, you and your mum *did brunch*," says Jas, impressed. "You're like society ladies now."

"Ha, hardly," I say, but I feel buoyed up a little. I definitely feel less like a criminal after some sleep and some food.

I cheer up even more once we're in the pool and we start practising handstands.

"Oh great, BUTTS are here," says Jas, as Mark and Liam bomb into the pool and we hear the familiar lifeguard whistle.

Jas smirks and looks at me expectantly, but when I don't react, she says, "Oh, I forgot, are they all your

best friends now?"

I open my mouth to respond, but then:

"Hey, Ella! Ella, over here!" shouts Gemma, waving, then jumping into the pool as well.

Before I can do or say anything, they all swim over to us, and start a splashing fight. Jas looks even *less* impressed, if that's at all possible.

"Wanna jump off the high board?" asks Liam.

"You guys go," says Jas. "We'll watch."

"Wasn't asking you, I was asking Ella," says Liam.

"Oh, um…" I pause.

"Ella never jumps off the high board," Jas explains for me.

"Why not?" asks Liam. "*Chicken?*"

"Everyone has different skills and is good at different things," says Jas protectively.

Normally, if ever Jas sticks up for me to people like Olivia, she's really dry and sarcastic. (And much cooler than me. Until I became super-good at confrontations, that is.) But something about these guys rattles her. She seems unnerved. So she sounds kind of goody-goody and pompous. Which is what they already think she is. So she's inadvertently meeting their expectations due to nervousness.

"*Everyone's good at different things,*" Gemma mimics unkindly.

"What are you good at? Ruining everyone's fun?" Liam chortles.

"No," I say without thinking. "Actually Jas totally helped me try to face my fear before. We got a book from the library about hypnotism and Jas tried to hypnotise me to not be scared of heights any more. But it didn't really work."

"Yeah. So, you guys, just *go*." Jas emphasises the *go* very clearly.

"Nah, we'll cure you!" enthuses Mark, grinning.

It's weird being in the pool with Mark now that I might fancy him.

Oh man, I totally forgot to look at his feet again last night. Now they're too hard to see again. I think they *might* be pointing at me.

"Yeah!" agrees Gemma.

"I *dare* you to jump off the high diving board," proclaims Liam.

"And I *double*-dare you," says Gemma.

"Triple," pipes up Mark.

"*AND*, uh, whatever four is," says Liam.

"Quadruple," Jas can't stop herself from supplying

tiredly.

"Yeah, I quadru— That one – dare you," says Liam.

"So now you have to, because it's a *dare*," states Gemma.

Mark grins his weirdly enchanting grin at me again. They start up a chant of "Do it! Do it!"

I beam and find myself considering it. I'm kind of getting swept along. Maybe it would be *fun*…? I mean, everyone seems to think I *can*…

"No! Look, *stop*!" Jas shouts them down. "Ella doesn't want to do it, and you can't make her."

Something about the way Jas says that annoys me. And I know that's really unfair, because she's just protecting me, which is really *nice*. But there's just some kind of *attitude* of hers creeping in there … about BUTTS. And for some reason it makes me want to prove her wrong.

"It's OK," I say grandly, "I'll do it!"

OH MY GOD. What am I *doing*? I sort of *come to* on the top step of the highest diving board (I don't know where I was before) and step forward.

I've had dreams like this. Maybe I'm asleep now. I

feel like I sleepwalked here. It was like I was proving a point and somehow it would be someone else's problem when I got to this bit. But it isn't. I'm still me. It's *my* problem. That delusion wasn't real. But this seems pretty real.

I often have that dream where I'm falling, and I wake as I land, so I feel like I'm landing in bed. I wake traumatised, sweaty and gasping for breath. But now, I'm about to do the awake version. Except I can't wake up and escape. Well, maybe in hospital?

Why didn't I start with the lowest board? I'm sweating as I creep along the board towards the end. What the hell is *wrong* with me? Why am I doing this? What even *was* the point I was trying to prove?

I peer over the edge and see Jas and my new BUTTS friends looking up at me. Gemma and Liam are grinning. Whatever I do next they will find entertaining: belly-flop, climbing cowardly back down... Jas looks worried. Mark waves and gives me a thumbs up. A shoot of excitement rises in my stomach in spite of everything. It would be cool to impress him. (But would it be *this* cool?) I look nervously back at the board...

I didn't *want* to start with the lowest board. Either

do something or don't do it, I'd thought. What's the point? Both boards are equally terrifying to me. Might as well do the one with the most kudos.

I remember Mum's *No Fear*-style proclamations about why she left, and about seizing life before you die, and never knowing if you would have been brave enough to do something if you don't try. I'm suddenly filled with anger. I don't know where it comes from. I'm *sick* of feeling scared and wretched. It's exhausting. *No more.* The anger fuels me. I think of all the people who are mean to me, and think I can't do things, and want me to fail. Well, guess what? I don't conform to expectations. I'm *free*.

I close my eyes and jump.

I'm falling for less than a second I think, then I splash down into the water.

It's *amazing*! That was *a-maz-ing*. I mean, it's probably because relief and/or adrenaline have flooded my body or whatever, but, oh my god, I think I'm high.

I climb out and see BUTTS whooping and cheering. "Go, Ella! Go, Ella!" shouts Gemma, doing a weird dance.

I grin and bow. "Let's do it again!" I yell.

OK, so it probably *is* my fault that I didn't notice Jas had got out of the pool. But also, it's *her* fault she left without saying goodbye. What's *that* about? I mean, I guess it's probably about her thinking I was ignoring her. But I wasn't; we were all hanging out together. Why does she have to be so sensitive?

"Hey, where are you?" I say, calling her when I get outside the pool.

"Home. What do you care?"

"I can't believe you're annoyed with me. That's so unfair."

"Of course it is, Ella," Jas replies sarcastically. "Everything that happens to you is, isn't it? You're just a victim. You never do anything wrong at all."

"What? Why are you being so horrible? You're the one that skulked off in a strop, without even saying goodbye."

"Oh yeah, cos you really care about manners and etiquette, don't you? After all the bombing and splashing you were doing?"

"We weren't hurting anyone. We were just having fun."

"Actually you scared a couple of kids, and you

were rude to that random old man."

"Well, *I* wasn't. But it *was* annoying that he was trying to swim lengths in the kids' bit. And anyway, he totally started it by tutting when we didn't move for him."

"Ella, he was really slow; he didn't want to swim in the lane because they were going so fast. It was unforgivably rude what Liam said to him."

"He probably didn't even hear." I start to feel guilty. Oh god.

"Whatever. I didn't want to be a part of it. I genuinely don't know what's happened to you."

"Nothing's happened! You're making this all sound worse than it is."

"Ella, I'm *worried* about you. *Really*. Think about what you're doing and why. Why are you suddenly hanging out with the horrible naughty kids? You used to hate how splashy they were in the pool; now you're doing it yourself. Don't you feel *bad*?"

"No," I say defiantly. "I was just having *fun*. I don't want to be a doormat any more. I want to live my life instead of watching other people live theirs and judging them."

"Oh, I'm *judging* people, am I?" Jas is suddenly

very haughty. "I tell you what, Ella, why don't you give me a call when you get this *rebel without a cause* nonsense out of your system and grow the hell up?" She hangs up.

"I have a cause!" I yell at my disconnected phone. I furiously text Jas.

> I HAVE A CAUSE thx.

That will show her.

She doesn't text back. Well, good. I don't need her anyway.

I definitely *do* need Jas. She's my best friend. Now I've calmed down a bit, I think I might be a tiny bit … *culpable*. I can't work out what went wrong. I'm confused. I wonder if I should just ring her and apologise for the hell of it, but part of me doesn't want to.

I *don't* need her. Do I?

Well, *fine*. If that's how she wants it to be, FINE. F-I-N-E. *FINE*.

I am just *fine** with this.

* *May not be completely fine.*

CHAPTER TWENTY-ONE

OMG, Jas is being really frosty with me at school on Monday! We're basically not speaking. Aaaagghhh. This is really weird. I hate it.

This is the longest we've fallen out since we both wanted the purple paint at the same time in reception class. Miss Brooker got us to take it in turns. I'm pretty sure our "row" lasted about five minutes at most. This is totally uncharted territory.

She's curt and polite when I ask her questions, but otherwise she's acting like she hates me. I want to cry and punch her at the same time. Well, I don't want to punch her; she's lovely. Aaaaagghh. No, she isn't. She's being very immature. Well, two can play that game.

OK, so two *can* play that game, but it turns out that one of us is *waaaay* better at it than the other.

As the week goes on, it seems like no skin off Jas's nose *at all* that we're barely speaking. But I am feeling really upset. And then really angry. It's fine. I said I was fine. We all know I was lying. But, still, FINE. Whatever.

"Ah, Ella, how was school today?" Dad appears to have been waiting for me in the kitchen when I get home from school on Friday. Radio 4 is burbling away in the background.

Well, let's see: Jas and I still aren't speaking, apart from when she took time out of her busy ignoring-me plan to comment that she thinks I should stop going on about having my bracelets nicked by a teacher, when actually that was a *private* conversation between me and Kaya.

Then there's this vague feeling of malaise I keep having, like I'm trapped – what's *that* about?

Also, I have *sort of* started craving the crazy fun I have with BUTTS even though it makes me feel guilty and terrible afterwards. It's like I forget the bad bits when things are dull.

"*Fine*," I tell him. "Kind of boring."

"Oh dear. Well, I was just making tea," says Dad.

"That's nice, Dad. I think I'm going to go upstairs and—"

"Nonsense!" interrupts Dad brightly. "Sit and have a cup of tea with your old dad. I've got bourbons." He proffers a plate of biscuits. It's *Jammie Dodgers* that I like. Why is it so hard for everyone to have all my favourite biscuits all the time?

I reluctantly sit at the kitchen table with him and sling my school bag on to the floor.

He hands me a cup of tea. "So," he says expectantly.

"So," I say crossly.

"So," he says again, and this time waves a hand expansively.

Well, this is annoying.

"So," I say again, and dunk a bourbon into my tea.

"Oh, is that nice?" Dad asks and copies me. He leaves his biscuit in too long, and some of it falls off into the tea.

"*Amateur*," I joke. "You have to do it quick like this," I demonstrate.

"I don't think I'll get it," he says. "They didn't have that in my day."

"Dad, I'm ninety per cent sure they had *dipping biscuits into tea* in your day."

"Well, maybe, but not in *our* house." Dad sips his tea. "It's nice to see you smiling."

I forcibly will myself not to roll my eyes. God, I find these kinds of conversations excruciating. "That's nice," I say deadpan.

"Nice to catch up, isn't it? I feel like I've hardly seen you lately," continues Dad.

"Mmm," I say non-commitally.

Please don't let him be ramping up to something. An intervention? He doesn't know I'm hanging with BUTTS. Surely not *the talk*?

There's a pause. We both look away. Each second is an hour long. "Nice tea," I say desperately to fill the silence.

OK, I'm properly annoyed now. I just want to go upstairs and have some *space*. Why is that so much to ask?

"Thanks. Hey, I was thinking maybe we could do something nice together this weekend? Perhaps go and see a film? Or see if Jas wants to come and go roller skating? Or you know, just *hang*?"

Dad does an attempt at a cool hand gesture as

he says *hang*. I am as embarrassed for him as I am irritated by it.

"I'm probably busy. P.S. Never say *hang* or do that gesture again," I order him crossly.

"You're just upset that your dad is so *rad*!" Dad does several more painfully uncool hand gestures, then finishes with, "*Word*."

I am momentarily speechless at the temerity of the man. My biscuit breaks and falls on the floor. *Great*, now I've lost a biscuit.

"*Idiot*," I tell the biscuit crossly. *Three-second rule?* No, it's wet from the tea. Dagnammit.

"What?" says Dad.

"My biscuit…" I reply sadly.

"Ella, did you just call me an idiot? Because that's very rude. I'm trying to be nice here," says Dad.

"Not *you*!" I gesture at the floor. "Please can I have another biscuit?"

"You know what, I'm getting sick of this attitude of yours," says Dad. "You treat this place like a hotel."

"How have we gone straight to that?" I ask him, bewildered.

"Well, you *do*," says Dad crossly. "A hotel with a free laundry service, and free biscuits."

ୠୠୠୠ↗

"But the biscuits were your idea!" I protest.

"You don't appreciate everything – or even *anything* I do for you round here."

"*What?*" I can't quite believe this is happening. I start to feel even more annoyed. "OK," I say sarcastically. "Well. Let the record show it's 4.43 p.m. and we have just made it to clichéd teenage–parent argument *Level Five*. Congratulations. I hope you're proud."

"I don't care," says Dad. "Maybe I should just stop doing everything. I bet you'd notice *then*."

"Oh, I *see*," I reply. "Are you threatening to go on laundry strike or something?"

"Yes," Dad says.

Annoyingly I think I might have just planted this idea in his head, and that wasn't necessarily where he was going with it. *Damn.*

"Well, that's just great, Dad," I tell him. "So what you're saying is hang out with me please or I'll stop doing your washing. Because that's actually blackmail."

Dad stares at me. He looks hurt, then angry, then lost for words. "Whatever," he finally says, and just gazes gloomily into the middle distance. I take it as my cue to leave.

I can't believe so much grief has been caused by a bourbon biscuit.

CHAPTER TWENTY-TWO

"Hi, Mum," I say. There's a long silence. "Mum…?" Does she even know she answered the phone? Is there such a thing as a *butt answer*?

"Hello, gorgeous! *No, over there! OVER THERE!* Not you, Ella."

"Um, cool. I'm just checking it's still OK for me to stay at your house again tonight? I can drop my bags off now to make it easier. There's loads of buses on Sat—"

"*Put it with this one!* Sorry, Ella. What?"

"I'm going to drop my stuff off at your flat now, if that's OK?"

"*Don't drill now! I'm on the phone!* Sorry, sweetheart, this is not a good time."

"I can call you back," I offer.

"No, I mean, it's not a good time to drop your bags off. I'm not home, as you can probably tell. *Wait two minutes!* Not you, Ella."

"You should have let me keep the key!" I try to sound light-hearted rather than accusatory.

"Well, I didn't know you'd be back so soon!" Is Mum's light-heartedness forced as well? Hard to tell on the phone.

"Don't suppose you keep a spare one under the mat or anything?" I venture.

"Are you mad?" retorts Mum. "I can't have anyone breaking in and stealing my fridge."

"Mum, I don't think even *Hercules* would be able to steal your fridge."

"Who?"

"He's an ancient Greek legend, famous for being strong and doing tasks. Twelve tasks. One was—"

"Oh no – *wait, WAIT*! Well, I don't want him to steal it either."

"OK, so, what time will you be back?"

"I don't know yet. I'll have to let you know later. This afternoon I've got back-to-back meetings."

"On a *Saturday*?"

"Yes. I'm twenty-four-seven, me, you know."

Mum sounds proud and boastful of this (to me) seemingly hellish situation. Who'd want to work on a *Saturday*?

"Do you want to have dinner together?" I suggest hopefully.

"I don't know, darling. I – *STOP! STOP!* I'll call you later. I have to go. Love you, bye." She hangs up before I have a chance to reply.

Well, OK. I can be adaptable. I'll just carry my bag around with me all day. That's fine. And luckily I have already taken my mum's advice and *streamlined* my new bag. I've only packed *one* library book (I just have to decide ahead of time what I'll feel like reading). And my tiny deodorant, wallet, pyjamas, Christmas-cracker comb, toothbrush and phone charger hardly weigh anything anyway. I'm light as a feather.

Not getting on with Jas does leave kind of a gap in my schedule, but I'm determined not to go crawling back to her when she's been so judgy and mean. So I pass time alone by walking around the mall and then head into Boots to try all the samples.

"Ella! *Psst,* Ella," I look up to see Gemma next to

me in the make-up aisle. "Watch this!" She winks and then puts the eyeshadow she's holding into her pocket.

"Did you just—?"

"*Shhhhh!*" Gemma interrupts. "Come on."

WHAT? Oh no. That didn't just happen... *Did it?* Numbly and in shock I follow Gemma out of Boots.

As we cross the threshold of the store I wince inwardly (and possibly outwardly) but nothing happens. We walk normally over to the fresh smoothie stand, where Mark and Liam are waiting on a bench.

"'Allo, 'allo." Mark grins at me.

I wave vaguely, still kind of numb and disorientated.

"Let's see then." Liam addresses Gemma. She shows him the tiny eyeshadow pot.

"*Meh.*" Liam is unimpressed. "That's *tiny*. Let's have a competition to see who can steal the *biggest* thing."

"Bigger things are tagged," says Gemma.

"Chicken," accuses Liam.

"Let's see you do it then." Gemma folds her arms.

"No problem." Liam disappears into Boots.

Oh god. What is *happening*? I mean, I know what's

happening, but still, what is *happening*?

Liam reappears a few minutes later and reveals a tiny can of deodorant.

Gemma bursts out laughing.

"It's still bigger than an eyeshadow," says Liam defensively.

"OK. Who's next?" Gemma turns to Mark and me.

"Wanna go together?" Mark smiles at me.

Um. Kinda. *What?* No, I mean, *no*, of course not. I'm definitely about to say no. Out loud … any second…

Mark offers me his arm in a sort of jokey chivalrous gesture. Like he's about to help me cross a puddle in the olden days. Before I know what I'm doing, I've threaded my arm through his, and we walk into Boots laughing together.

This Boots is massive. It has a mall entrance, where we are now, and a bus stop entrance on the next floor down. It's probably *too big* for anyone to notice shoplifters, isn't it? I mean, probably…

Oh god, *shoplifters*. *Shoplifters will be prosecuted*. That's the main thing I know about shoplifters.

"Cheaper stuff is better," says Mark quietly, as he leads us around the store. "Some of the pricier stuff is tagged." I nod dazedly, as if I am listening to a new scientific theory that I don't understand, but is probably true.

Mark finds a deodorant that is slightly bigger than Liam's, but still untagged, and slips it into his pocket.

"Your bag is *perfect* for this," Mark tells me as we carry on walking round, pressed up against each other. "You could win. Shall I help you find something really big?"

I nod mutely. *What in the hell is wrong with me?* I can't believe I'm so excited to be linking arms with Mark that I'm considering *shoplifting*. This is *insane*. But also nice and warm and fuzzy. And exciting.

I guess I just never had a *bad boy* think I was *cool* before. Or anyone think I was cool *ever* really. Even Jas would affectionately tease me for being a nerdy geek. Even though she is one too. The hypocrite.

But everyone else I know is so good. There's something crazy and liberating about doing this. I feel a bit like I'm trying on a different lifestyle to see if it's for me. I mean, it *definitely* won't fit me, and I could end up in prison. But I won't know that for sure until I try it on, will I?

Can't I just shut the sensible nagging voice in

my head up for five minutes? I mean, nothing bad happened when I did that and jumped off the diving board, did it? (Apart from falling out with Jas and completely losing my best friend.) (*No*. Not my fault.) *Hmmm*...

"Hairbrushes," I hear myself say.

"Eh?"

"Hairbrushes are big, and I don't *think* they're tagged. Not all of them, anyway."

"Cool," says Mark and we investigate the hair section, finding the biggest, non-tagged brush we can find. We look this way and that, and then I slip it into my bag.

Mark feels my sudden, panicked pull on his arm. "Don't run," he says quietly. "We have to walk calmly, or it's suspicious."

OMG, OMG, OMG. We walk crazily slowly towards the exit. I'm definitely sweating too much.

As we cross the threshold of the store, I feel a rough hand on my shoulder. "Excuse me, miss."

I scream and drop my bag.

Laughter. I'm surrounded by laughter. Liam and Gemma are in hysterics.

"Ahahahahaha! Gotcha!" Liam is doubled over.

Even Mark looks amused as he tries to guide everyone out of the way of the shop entrance. "Very funny," he says tiredly, picking up my bag and carrying it, as we head back to the bench.

"Your face!" Liam points at me, still laughing helplessly. "Priceless!"

"*Excuse me, miss.*" Gemma does Liam's voice. "I can't believe you *screamed*!" She bursts out laughing again.

"Best. Prank. Ever," declares Liam gleefully.

"I wish we'd filmed it," Gemma laments, still laughing.

As my breathing returns to normal, it sinks in that Liam just impersonated a security guard and properly scared the *hell* out of me. I start laughing as well, mainly out of *relief*. My knees feel weak and I sit on the bench.

Oh my god. That was *terrifying*. I feel lucky I didn't actually wee.

Gemma claps me on the back, mistaking my laughter for appreciation of their wit, when really it's a hysterical reaction. I do *not* appreciate their wit. I want to *kill* them.

"Right, who won?" asks Liam, as they all calm

down and finally stop laughing. Everyone puts their spoils on the bench next to me. My hairbrush is easily the biggest item.

"No way! Newbie scream-face won!" Liam sounds equally annoyed and impressed. "Well, I'm definitely going to win round two."

"Are you kidding?" asks Mark. "You just caused a massive commotion. We can't go back in there for *ages*. People are still looking at us."

We look around. It does feel like there are adults everywhere frowning at us, but then it sort of always does. All you really have to do is wear a hoody and adults frown at you in the mall. But *still*.

"All right, let's go and get chips or something and then come back," says Gemma. "You coming, Ella?"

"Ummm … no, I have to meet my friend soon," I lie. I'm actually not sure I can stand up yet.

We say our goodbyes and I watch them disappear down an escalator.

Oh god, *I stole*. I look at the hairbrush sitting next to me on the bench and feel sick. What is *wrong* with me?

I hate feeling this guilty. It's horrible. *Go away, guilty feeling.*

I drink some of my bottle of water and try to feel better.

I don't feel better.

OK. I know. I will *return* this hairbrush! I don't need it. I already have a hairbrush. And a cracker comb. I'm all set.

I go back into Boots and pop the hairbrush back on the shelf. *There.* I'm a genius. No harm done. Or at least, all harm that was done *undone.* Just like how eating an apple cancels out eating two Galaxy bars. Everyone knows that. Me and the universe are quits.

CHAPTER TWENTY-THREE

I get to Mum's flat at 5 p.m., just like she told me to, but she's still not back. She's not answering her phone either. I hang around for five minutes, then go to the café down the road, and text her that I'm waiting.

The café were clearly hoping they could close early, and seem slightly annoyed they now have one customer scuppering this plan. They do reluctantly serve me, though, emphasising that they're shutting at six.

"Oh, don't worry, I'll be long gone by then," I say.

It's five to six. All the other chairs are up on the tables. I am very much still here. My mum is not replying to any of my calls, texts, or WhatsApps. The last waitress is sweeping the floor near me, looking decidedly unimpressed.

I mean, I'm not an expert on body language (I keep forgetting to look at Mark's feet, for one thing). But I think it's fair to say she *definitely* wants me to leave.

"You need to leave," she tells me. *Nailed it*. Maybe I'm better at reading body language than I thought.

"Um, yes, I'll be going soon," I say.

"I need to lock up. Some of us have homes to go to."

"Me too," I tell her pointlessly.

Technically I have *two* of them. So, *ha*, in your face grumpy waitress lady with a legitimate desire to finish work. *Eugh*.

She scowls at me. So *this* is what it feels like to make a complete stranger hate you. Good to know. Normally only people that know me get to do that. I'm really branching out today.

I ring Mum again but no answer.

I let the waitress crossly chuck me out and walk back to Mum's flat. It's starting to get pretty dark. The only other thing nearby that's open is a pub at the other end of the street, and I can't go in there. My normal house (Dad's) is on the other side of town. It would take an hour to walk it, and almost as long on the bus as I'd have to change. Maybe forty-five minutes? And maybe Mum will be back in five minutes…?

I walk back to Mum's and sit on the front step. I decide to read my library book using my phone as a torch. I finish it in ten minutes. I forgot I was so near the end. I don't have any other library books to read because I only packed one. I have nothing to read now. Damn my *streamlining*. And my feet hurt because I don't normally wear my *Jay-Shees* with these socks, and for some reason now they're rubbing. But I don't have any plasters. Why don't I have plasters? I usually *always* have plasters. I take my shoes off and rub my feet, then put them back on. They sting anew. I totally could have put just two or three plasters in my bag just in case. I didn't need a *whole box*. Plasters are tiny, they take up no room at all. I'd still have been *streamlined*.

I sit there for a moment pondering how I've managed to lurch from one extreme to the other, and that actually I'm neither of my parents, and perhaps I need to find some kind of middle ground that works for *me*. But then I am distracted from this thought by the noise of some men laughing on their way to the pub. I don't think they see me, but I suddenly feel very vulnerable and afraid.

By half six I am still sitting anxiously on the step, bored of clicking refresh on my phone when nothing new is happening on it, starting to get cold, and feeling pretty annoyed with my mum. I get that she's busy, but *still*. She *said* she wanted to make it up to me. She *said* she missed me. But maybe this is exactly what I should expect from someone who could vanish from my life so completely?

At six forty-five, with still no word from Mum, my phone battery about to die, and no way of charging it, I feel distinctly unsafe. It's properly dark now. I'm totally alone and I'm about to lose my lifeline with the world.

I feel like I've been abandoned all over again. Maybe I should use my last bit of battery to ask my dad to come and pick me up?

A taxi pulls up. Mum staggers out of it carrying loads of shopping bags.

"Oh my god, I'm SO SORRY!" she shouts down the path at me, struggling to shut the taxi door and pay her driver. She stumbles towards me. "Oh god, darling, this is the saddest sight I've ever seen." She means me, sitting forlornly on her front step.

Maybe I should feel relieved, but instead I burst into angry tears. I'm so angry. *Be cool, be cool*, I tell myself. *Don't say anything to scare her away.*

"I *hate* you!" I hear myself scream. "Why do you keep doing this to me?" Then I sob uncontrollably, and Mum leads me into her flat.

Oh yeah. Pretty cool.

I think I cry for about ten minutes. I'm sure that's probably what *Wonder Woman* would have done. Proper blotchy-faced, snotty, undignified wailing.

Mum sits me at her kitchen table and gives me a glass of water, and occasionally pats my arm to comfort me, but basically lets me cry until I start to run out of steam. Once I'm at the intermittent hiccupping stage she sits down at the table as well.

"Darling, I am *so sorry*," she says earnestly. "Everything ran late. I couldn't stop it."

"I – hic – rang – hic – you," I say.

"I'm *so sorry*. I knew I was late, so I was focused on trying to get everything done quickly. I didn't even look at my phone."

My hiccups are receding. I drink some water. "You have to tell people when you're running *that* late, Mum – hic. That's *insane*. I'm – hic – *thirteen*. All alone outside on your street."

"I know, I know," says Mum. "I'm an idiot. I've cut you a key now. Your own one."

"Great," I say flatly.

"Ella, I'm—"

"You're sorry, *I know*," I interrupt crossly. (*What am I doing?*) "It's so easy to just say sorry, isn't it?" I accuse her. "It doesn't erase things."

Well. If I'm *going* to scare Mum away, I might as well do it properly I guess. *In for a penny, in for a pound.* Also I can't seem to stop talking.

"But—" begins Mum and I interrupt her again.

"*Oh, I've never been abroad, so I'd better go off to start a business, and leave my kid.*" I do a sarcastic impression of Mum. "*Oh, it's taking longer than one second, well, I guess I'd better do up my new flat and still ignore my daughter. Oh, now I want to see her again, but only for five minutes if I absolutely have to.*"

"That's not—"

"You *said* you wanted a proper relationship with

me, but you *don't*. You don't want to do anything with me that conflicts with your *precious schedule*."

OK. I seem to have finished. Well, that ought to do it.

"Ella?" Mum begins cautiously.

"Yes?"

"You know when you said you understood why I had to leave…? Was that a … fib?"

"Maybe!" I say, defensively. "I just didn't want you to leave again. I thought that's what you wanted me to say. But no, I'm not just *fine* with it, Mum. I do *want* to forgive you, but I can't."

Mum suddenly wraps me in a giant hug. She sort of flings herself at me and the table wobbles. "Thank you for being honest with me," she whispers tightly into my hair.

"OK," I say dumbly. It *is* a nice hug I suppose.

Mum finally pulls back. "My therapist says we can always build on new beginnings based on honesty."

Wait, *what*? "You're in therapy?"

"Yeah, it's been really good," says Mum.

I'm stunned. "What does your therapist say about your timekeeping?"

"That it's not cool."

"Your therapist uses the phrase 'not cool'?"

"No, I'm paraphrasing," says Mum. "She uses the word 'paraphrasing', though. That's where I learnt it. It means saying the same thing in different words. It's a great word, isn't it?"

"Um… I guess?"

"I'm learning so many things now, Ella. Things I never thought possible." (Jeez, dare to dream, Mum – it was always possible to learn the word "paraphrasing".) "I'm in a much better place. And I'm going to learn to be a much better mum. I know I've got some making up to do. I thought we could start here…"

Mum reaches for the shopping bags. "OK, so part of the reason I was late was I went shopping… I do want a proper relationship with you. But you're right, I've got a little bit used to being able to do my own thing. Anyway…"

Mum tips out a bag on to the table. "I thought we could watch a movie tonight so I've got microwave popcorn, ice cream, chocolate, crisps…" She empties out another bag. "Oh, and I picked this up for you," she says, as a jumper and a top and a dress tumble out. "I thought they'd suit you."

"Wow," I say.

Mum smiles, delighted. "Wait, there's more…" She's bought me make-up and some special bathroom stuff for me to leave at her flat and some really silly but cute pyjamas and slippers.

"This is really nice," I say, only partly out of politeness.

"And…" Mum passes me a Chinese takeaway menu, "let's order everything!"

"Really?" I say.

"Yes!" Mum beams. "I'm going to have a night off and hang out and have fun with *my daughter*!"

We do order nearly everything on the menu. It's AMAZING. Then we change into our pyjamas and bring Mum's duvet into the living room, and sit on her sofa, and watch two films with Melissa McCarthy in them because we love her, and eat what feels like every kind of junk food in the world. It's so fun and snuggly. I feel much better.

CHAPTER TWENTY-FOUR

When I arrive home on Sunday evening I immediately realise something is different. Dad is nowhere to be seen but evidence of his last movements is everywhere. He clearly hasn't waited for me to have his Sunday-night crumpets. Well, that's fine. I can easily put crumpets in the toaster *myself*. Is this supposed to be a *punishment*? Hah. Nice try, Dad.

In fact, if anything this is a *double* win for me: now instead of having to sit through another awkward dinner conversation with my dad, I can take these up to my room and watch YouTube videos on my computer. Heh.

I sit on my bed and get my laptop out. Something is definitely different, but I can't put my finger on what right away. I've nearly finished eating when I realise there are no clean, ironed school shirts hanging on my wardrobe door, waiting to be put away. *Oh*. And no clean pile of clothes on my bed. OK.

I go over to my laundry basket and it is still full of all my dirty clothes from the week. *I see*. Dad is making a *point*. Well, great. *Honestly*. I can't help but feel this is very immature and petty of him.

I mean, *I'm* a very mature person now; I have *psychologist-approved-honest* conversations with my previously absent mother. I'm so above these petty mind games. But I will maybe just have to *very quickly* play one petty mind game, just to prove how petty they are, and that I can still win. I'll show him. This is at best a minor inconvenience. I can easily do my *own* washing. I'm basically a grown-up after all.

I carry my washing downstairs and find my dad watching TV in the living room. He's ignoring me, or at least pretending to ignore me. This is like Jas all over again. *Eurgh*. Why is everyone terrible except me?

"Well done," I say in an admittedly slightly juvenile manner.

"Oh." Dad looks up, then back to the TV. "Hello,

194

Ella," he says dismissively. I bet he *practised* looking that laid-back and lounging in his chair.

"I can do my *own* washing," I say. "I mean, if *you* can do it, I'm sure it's *easy*."

"Great, go ahead." Dad doesn't even look up this time.

"Great. I'm going," I say.

"*Going?* The washing machine's in the *kitchen*." Dad allows himself a little chortle. "Oh *dear*, you *might* find it tricky if you don't even know where the washing machine *is*."

Ughh. Parent cliché jokes. "*They don't even know where the washing machine is!*" *Ha ha ha ha ha.*

Like it's *our* fault we spend the first ten years of our lives banned from touching anything in case we have sticky fingers, and then suddenly we're supposed to just *know* how everything works.

OK. Deep breath. Rise above this. He's baiting you, so you'll shout at him and then he can ground you. Keep it cool.

"Yeah, well, I don't want to use your stupid washing machine," I quickly counter. Ha. He didn't expect that. Admittedly neither did I. Why did I say that?

"Oh? Are you going to use the sink?" Dad snorts laughter.

"*No*," I reply crossly. "I'm going to go to Mum's to use *her* washing machine."

"Don't be silly." Dad glances up at me, then back to the TV. "Just sling your stuff into the machine." (Ha, I've got him on the ropes! He's backing down and being *helpful*.) "If you want, I'll even show you how it works." (Hmmm. That *is* nice of him actually.)

Part of me is now thinking "Oh, thank goodness, I really can't be bothered going out again." But another part of me is thinking, "I've won! He's backing down. He thinks he's made his point, but I should teach him not to mess with me..." I wonder which side of me will –

"No!" I hear myself yell. "I don't need your help! I'm going to Mum's!"

"Sure you are," says Dad sarcastically.

Uh-oh. I've lost the higher ground. He thinks I'm bluffing. And I *am*. Aren't I? God, petty mind games are exhausting.

"I *mean* it," I threaten anticlimactically.

He lets it hang there for a moment. "*Whatever*."

How *dare* he call my bluff? I was just enjoying the coming-of-age film of my life that's running in my head and he's ruining it.

"Second thoughts?" Dad glances at me a bit *too* gleefully for my liking.

"Nope!" I grab my bag of washing and my coat that still has my wallet in it, and head out before I can change my mind.

∞∞∞

Coming-of-age film of my life is back on, I think determinedly, as I march down the street. A bus is coming as I get near the bus stop, so I run and just make it. *Phew*. See? Things are looking up *already*.

There's always a good running-for-a-bus scene in most films. This whole Dad-being-unhelpful-with-washing thing is just some adversity I have to rise above... And then there'll probably be a montage scene where Mum and I drink coffee while my washing washes. And then we high-five at the end. Simple as.

As I try to envisage this scene, I realise I can't actually picture a washing machine at Mum's flat. That's weird. It must be under the—

SHE DOESN'T HAVE A WASHING MACHINE.

I jolt as the bus goes over a bump. OMG. I feel a mild surge of panic. Mum doesn't *have* a washing machine. Instead, she uses some random service that comes and collects dirty clothes, dry-cleans them, then delivers them back a few days later. She has an app for it on her phone.

PHONE! The bus jolts over another bump. *I DON'T HAVE MY PHONE!* The bus brakes suddenly and there's a loud beep. I'm momentarily thrown to the side and bounce off the window.

I don't have my phone! It's charging in my bedroom. A cold sweat breaks out at the back of my neck and my panic level rises significantly. I just ran out of the house without my phone. I don't mean to overreact, but this is the worst thing that has ever happened to anyone ever.

It's like I've forgotten my legs. It's a *part* of me. I don't think I've ever left the house without my phone before. I mean, maybe once, when I was a baby…

OK. Don't panic. Don't *panic*. Let's review the situation: I am on a bus. The bus is heading into town. I can't tell Mum I am coming. I can't tell Dad I don't have my phone.

I *suppose* the *obvious* thing to do would be to get

off the bus at the next stop and go home again, tell Dad that Mum doesn't have a washing machine and then just let him help me do my washing under a cloud of shame and defeat.

But why *should* I? Dad will be so smug. I can't bear it.

If this *was* a film, this would be the bit where my fairy godmother appears, or I find out I'm a wizard. Either of those things would actually be very helpful.

I'm nearly all the way into town. The bus is now speeding past shops and I stare glumly and mindlessly at chemists, kebab shops and launderettes…

Hey! *Hang on a minute, lads, I've got a great idea.* I press the stop button and scramble out at the next stop.

I can take my clothes to a *launderette*! If no fairy godmothers are going to save me (from mild humiliation with my dad) then I will just have to save *myself*.

∽∂∂∂∂↘

OK, I don't want to boast, but I am a *natural* at using the launderette. I mean, luckily they have a change machine and I think the washing powder they sell seems a bit expensive but otherwise it's all gone really smoothly. My washing got clean and I put it in a dryer. *Smooth*.

This could all still totally be a scene in my film anyway. Though I have no one to high-five. And time definitely drags without a phone or a book. Even when you are starring in a film in your head.

I sit on one of the handy (but hard and uncomfortable) chairs, waiting for my washing to be dry, and try very hard not to make eye contact with the old man opposite me who seems to be muttering to his fist like it's a person. I wonder idly if he used to have a ventriloquist act in his youth. Then he starts pacing the room and trying to talk to inanimate objects. I start to worry that if he realises I'm real, he'll talk to me.

The dryer beeps and I stick my hand in. The washing's still a bit damp. *Hmmm*. Should I put another 20p in?

"I never trusted you!" the old man rants at the change machine in the corner.

OK, *fine*. I admit it. I'm a *tad* scared. But he's probably harmless.

The old man kicks the change machine and hops about swearing. It's still *probably* fine, though. OK, now he's just told it to "Come outside and say that."

I stay very still, crouched down by my dryer, and try not to panic, as the old man punches the machine, and gets even angrier. It is at this moment that my dad *and my mum* suddenly barge into the launderette.

Oh, thank god. I mean … what are *they* doing here? I'm obviously *fine*.

"There you are!" cries Dad. "What the hell do you think you're doing?"

From the corner of my eye I see the old man spin round in shock, and flatten himself against the wall next to the change machine.

"My washing, *obviously*." I stand up. "What are you both doing here? *Together?*"

"I was really worried about you, you absolute idiot!" shouts Dad. "I thought you'd gone to your mum's! I rang her to see if you wanted a lift back!"

"Oh," I say.

"Yes, *oh*," says Dad coldly. "We couldn't think where you'd be and we were just about to call the *police*. Then I wondered if you'd be daft enough to try to find a launderette. And look at that – *daft* – just like your mother for not having a washing machine in the first place."

Mum coughs indignantly. "We're supposed to present a united front, remember?"

"Yes, well." Dad attempts to calm himself. It's weird. He never normally gets angry, but once he *is* angry, he can't seem to stop. "It was your mother's idea, too."

"We'd have been here sooner if your dad didn't slow down for *every single speed bump*," adds Mum.

"What happened to our united front?" asks Dad.

Mum shrugs and turns to me. "What were you *thinking*? And why didn't you answer your phone?" she demands.

"Oh-ho," I respond sarcastically, "you want to talk about answering your phone all of a sudden, do you?" Then I cough the word "doorstep" into my hand.

"Well, it's good to see you being cheeky to your mum as well as to me," says Dad.

"We really need to work on this united-front thing," Mum tells him.

"Get your stuff," instructs Dad.

"It's not dry yet," I tell him.

"Do it!" replies Dad firmly.

"Your dad doesn't get upset about much, Ella,

so when he does, I suggest you listen to him," says Mum.

"Thank you," Dad tells her politely.

"Nice united front, guys," I say.

"Put a sock in it, Ella," says Mum.

Ugh. Where do they get these phrases? I forget that Mum is only cool compared to Dad. She's not actually cool.

But I can't help but grin to myself as I retrieve my damp washing from the dryer and scramble it back into my laundry bag.

CHAPTER TWENTY-FIVE

Get this. Mum stays for a cup of tea once we're back at Dad's house. (Well, instant coffee that she is sniffy about.) But *still*. They can stand to be in the same room together. They're actually sort of bonding over how "naughty" I was.

I wasn't *naughty*. Because:

(a) I am not four.

(b) It was an accident that I forgot my phone.

And I maintain Dad had technically said I *could* go to Mum's (even though he said it sarcastically) and if anything, it's all *his* fault for being mean about my washing. And Mum's fault for not having a washing machine. But no one wants to have a long, hard look in the mirror, do they? *Hypocrites*.

"Uh-oh," Dad comments, as I tip my damp laundry

on to the floor by the dryer, near where him and Mum are sitting at the kitchen table.

"What do you mean 'uh-oh'?" I ask.

"Did you wash all your dark colours together with the whites?" Dad sips his tea.

Mum stifles an amused snorting noise into her cup. *Not helpful.*

What is their problem? *Hmmm*, is my white school shirt a bit darker? Like kind of grey? Or am I imagining it?

"I was kind of in a hurry," I say crossly, to cover the fact it didn't occur to me that this was a bad idea, despite having recently watched that episode of *The Simpsons* where Bart puts his red cap in the white washing and dyes Homer's shirt pink.

Mum and Dad are *rubbish* at hiding how funny they find this.

"It's like that time she drew a moustache on herself when she was six," giggles Mum. "Do you remember? We couldn't get it off straight away, so she had to go to school like it?"

Dad chuckles. "Oh yes! Also, it's a bit like that time when she wanted that *Supergirl* T-shirt, so she took your expensive blue top and drew on it?"

"No, that wasn't funny," says Mum.

"I think it was the same pen. Why didn't we take it off her?" muses Dad.

"What am I going to do?" I interrupt.

Dad comes over to investigate. "We'll leave the shirts soaking overnight with some bleach. But you'll have to wear a grey one tomorrow."

"What? Noooooo!" I whimper.

"I think it's the best we can do," says Dad kindly but sadly. "Maybe don't run off like a lunatic and these things wouldn't happen."

I sigh.

"Tell you what," says Mum, downing her coffee. "Why don't I give you a quick make-up tutorial with that new flicky eyeliner I bought you? Then you can do that tomorrow to detract from the greyness? Maybe no one will even notice?"

Later, in my room, I feel strangely emotional and have an overwhelming urge to talk to Jas. I could call her. But what if she doesn't answer her phone? I can't even remember why we started arguing. Oh yeah, she was judgy about me at the swimming pool. But maybe in a way, she wasn't. Could I have got it wrong?

I try to look at the facts and sort them in my mind:

Fact 1 – Jas is the loveliest person ever. But her family are wonderful, so it's *easy* for her to be lovely. If anything, it's almost *cheating*.

Fact 2 – I am quite a nice person too, but it's harder for me, as my parents are nuts.

Fact 3 – I had genuine fun in the pool being splashy with BUTTS.

Fact 4 – Jas said I was rude and mean to people around me. (I hate this fact; it makes me feel terrible and hypocritical. And this is what is making me so resentful towards her, I realise.)

But Jas wouldn't *lie* to me (see Fact 1, she is too lovely). So either, I had fun that was technically mean of me; *or ... or ...* Jas is *mistaken*! And she just takes splashing, and other things, too seriously.

That's OK then. We just have a difference of opinion. We'll have to agree to disagree. I'll try not to rub in her face all the new fun stuff I'm doing, in the same way I wouldn't keep offering peanuts to people with nut allergies. That way everyone can be happy.

I probably can't tell Jas she's mistaken, because

part of the problem is she can't see it. So I'll just apologise for the stuff I have done wrong… I mean, maybe I was a *bit* splashy…

I start crafting a text. I want to sincerely apologise, but carefully avoid admitting *all* the guilt. It turns into a bit of an essay. I read it back. I think my English teacher would say there are too many "buts" and emojis. I send it anyway.

I get a response from Jas immediately. That was quick! Nervously and excitedly I grab my phone.

Jas has simply replied,

> tl;dr

Followed by

> *Smiley winky face sticking its tongue out.*

I laugh in spite of myself.

> Very funny!

I type back.

> Reading it now

She sends back.

It would be quicker to just ring her. I should just…

She rings me.

"Who is this?" I answer.

We both laugh and insult each other and are friends pretty much straight away. It's such a relief. Jas even thinks she was a *bit* stubborn too. Result!

I relax and tell her all about the launderette and my mum and everything. She is sympathetic but also accuses me of never learning. Which I think is unfair. But I don't *really* care because it's just so great to be friends again.

"I have to go," says Jas finally.

"Cool. Well, see you tomorrow. I'll be the one in the grey shirt."

Jas chuckles. "Maybe no one will even notice?"

CHAPTER TWENTY-SIX

"Ella Hudson! My office now!" Miss Gaskew shouts across the entrance hall, as I fail to camouflage myself among the throng of pupils entering the school on Monday morning.

I reluctantly follow Miss Gaskew down the staffroom corridor, and wait outside her office door for a moment, so we can go through the pantomime of her telling me to enter, even though she knows I'm there.

"Ella." Miss Gaskew is sitting at her desk as I come in, looking up at me expectantly. "Why do you think I have called you into my office this time?"

"I'm going to go out on a limb and guess that it's my shirt," I say.

"Very good." Does a flicker of amusement cross

her face? Can't be sure.

"So." She pauses. "Why are you wearing a non-regulation school shirt?"

"Well, obviously I didn't *mean* to," I tell her. "I had a mishap with my washing. I was trying to prove to my dad that I could do it myself, because he's been a bit weird since my mum came back. But now they seem to be getting on actually. But anyway, I mixed up the colours, and it was an accident."

Miss Gaskew's face remains passive, but she says, "Oh dear, Ella, I'm sorry to hear that."

"Sorry enough to give me my bracelets back?" I attempt to joke.

Miss Gaskew stares at me. For a moment I think she's working up to seriously shout at me. Then she says, "OK. Just this once."

Wait, *WHAT*?

She unlocks a drawer of her desk, roots around, and hands me the brown envelope with my name on. Miss Gaskew is *nice*! Miss Gaskew has a nice side. Did she just take *pity* on me because of *grey-shirt-gate*?

"Oh my *god*, thank you so much!" I splutter.

"There are no gods in here that require invoking,"

responds Miss Gaskew stiffly.

"Sorry, Miss," I reply hastily.

"Tell NO ONE I did this," she instructs.

"Of course," I reply earnestly. I pause. "Can I tell Jas?" I hear myself ask idiotically. *Obviously not, you moron.*

Miss Gaskew stares at me again. I'm worried she's about to ask for the envelope back. But instead she says, *"Tell her what?"* and leaves a beat, to make sure I catch her meaning. Her mouth twitches in what could *almost* be a smile.

Oh my god! This is *incredible*. I'm involved in a cover-up with a teacher! Not just any teacher – the scariest teacher in the *whole school*. Ha! *What gold that went missing?* Nothing to see here, your honour. It never happened. Erased from existence. Wink, wink, nudge, nudge, say no more. Amazing.

"We are *clear* on this school's jewellery policy, aren't we, Ella?" says Miss Gaskew.

"Yes, Miss. Very clear," I say humbly. "Um, bye. Thanks." And I quickly leave her office before I accidentally undo any of the magic that just happened.

"Oi, grey shirt!"

"Excuse me, did you know your shirt is grey?" (Laughter.)

The canteen really is a hotbed of older kids making the same observations over and over again. I've fallen back on my old tactic of pretending to be deaf when people are clearly talking to me.

Did Miss Gaskew give me my bracelets back as compensation because she could predict the bullying I was likely to receive for the rest of the day? If so, I am grateful. I can pretend they're a little talisman protecting me from insults. (From my pocket. I'm not putting them on – I'm not an *idiot*.) Well, not a total idiot anyway.

I swore Jas to secrecy when I told her about Miss Gaskew, and she was really impressed. Every now and then she says, "I still can't believe it."

❦❦❦❦

"I still can't believe it," says Jas as we file into art, after lunch.

"*I know*," I agree for the umpteenth time.

It's understandable we're still in shock that Miss Gaskew is only *pretending* to be evil to maintain order. It's kind of like a *Twilight Zone* twist. *It was Earth all along! Bruce Willis is a ghost! Miss Gaskew has a nice side!* (OK, maybe it's not *quite* that exciting, but that just shows how boring school normally is, that that's how it *feels*.)

"Nice *shirt*!" Olivia smirks and knocks into me as she files past us into the art room. Sasha and Grace giggle.

"*Hack*," I mutter under my breath. I mean, come on. Upwards of thirty people have come up with that exact material. Not even a joke, just an observation.

"Settle down! Settle down!" Mrs Wiggins has moved the tables together into one giant one. We all have to sit round the edge facing the household objects she has placed in the middle, which we will be drawing with charcoal.

Once she's issued her instructions, Mrs Wiggins disappears into the tiny room next door where the clay oven is.

Mrs Wiggins spends most of her time in there, drinking tea and talking to Mrs Peters, who has similarly abandoned her art class on the other side of the tiny room.

They only really come out and teach if we get too loud. There's kind of this understanding that this is a

214

sweet deal for all concerned, so everyone generally behaves and enjoys the doss.

"Oh, Ella, I really like your eye make-up," says Fiona, as we all start sketching.

Fiona is one of those lovely, inoffensive people that don't seem to have any enemies. She's clever, but never bullied for it, and because she's kind of trendy, I take this as a huge compliment.

"Oh, thanks," I smile. "My mum showed me how to do it."

Fiona smiles back. "Your eyes really pop. How did you do the flick? Will you show me?"

"Yeah, sure, of course."

"Oh my god, you can't be *serious*." Olivia Jones has heard this exchange from a few seats away, and is apparently enraged by it.

Most people carry on shading in their household objects, but some people stop and look up with interest.

That's the thing about art, when all the tables are put into one big one like this, so we're all facing the middle, everyone can pretty much hear everyone else's conversations.

"Sorry?" Fiona looks confused at Olivia.

"You can't *possibly* want make-up tips from this *fashion reject*?" Olivia points at me, incensed. "Look at her. She's so boring her personality has even turned her shirt grey." Sasha and Grace splutter laughter and a few other people chuckle.

"Hey," Jas objects on my behalf.

My grey shirt makes me feel weirdly exposed and insecure, like I've forgotten how to stick up for myself. *Must try harder*...

"I'm just saying what we're all thinking." Olivia raises her hands in fake surrender.

"But, Olivia," I force myself to say brightly, "I thought it was *your* bag that says *UGLY COW* on it? Or is that just a *coincidence*?"

There is some shocked laughter from the people in earshot. People aren't even hiding that they're staring at Olivia to see what she'll do now.

Olivia looks at me surprised, then her eyes narrow. "Oh my god. It was *you*, wasn't it?" she accuses. "You're going to pay for this!"

"I don't know what you mean," I reply breezily.

"You *vandalised* my bag!" she hisses.

"Well, if someone thinks you're so ugly it's worth writing it on your bag, maybe you should think twice before you go around bullying people just because they've never used a launderette before." I try to sound sage, but that last bit kind of got away from me. I sense I'm losing the crowd.

"*What?*" Olivia shakes her head, as if to clear it, then says, "I can prove it was you, you know."

"*How?*" Gemma from BUTTS a few seats away suddenly pipes up.

I glance around the room. Wow, even more people than I realised are listening. I dart a quick, nervous look at Mark. He smiles at me, and a little surge of excitement goes through me, despite feeling worried about what Olivia will say next.

Olivia possibly feels ganged up on; she looks flustered, but she continues. "I can totally prove Ella did it," she states. "She has means, motive and opportunity."

Mark snorts laughter from across the room. "Oh, this'll be good."

Olivia is being attacked from all sides. This is unusual. (For her.)

"Keep out of it!" She glares at Mark, and tries to regain her cool. "Ella owns Tippex – *means*."

"We all own Tippex," interrupts Liam.

"Yeah, that's circumstantial," agrees Mark, smirking.

"I'm still talking," protests Olivia.

"Go on then," scoffs Gemma.

"She, uh, was alone in the form room that lunch – *opportunity*."

"She wasn't alone," Mark says.

"*What?*" Olivia is so not used to being interrupted this much.

"She wasn't alone. I had detention that day too."

"*And.*" Olivia decides to just soldier on. "She was annoyed I got her detention by telling on her for wearing bracelets – *motive*."

"*Wait* – so you *admit* you snitched on Ella and deliberately got her detention?" says Gemma.

There's sort of a shocked gasp around the room.

"When you have those *exact* bracelets?" says Fiona, surprised. "You're wearing them right *now*."

Olivia touches her wrist uncomfortably.

Gemma folds her arms, satisfied. "I think you owe Ella an apology."

Olivia makes a frustrated scream noise in the back of her throat. "Look, this has nothing to do with you," she tells Gemma heatedly.

"Yes, it does, you sneaky *snitch*," replies Gemma. "Setting people you don't like up for detention like some kind of *bent copper*!"

"Yeah!" says Liam.

"I hate to break it to you, but loads of people don't like you," says Gemma. "Literally anyone could have written that on your bag. *I* could have done it."

Olivia starts to look wounded and vulnerable. *No.* I refuse to feel sorry for her. She's *horrible.*

"Yeah!" Liam is enjoying this. "*I* could have done it."

"Guys, guys," I interrupt, "we don't need to go all *I'm Spartacus* about this." (Especially as I *am* guilty of this particular crime, I don't add.)

"What's 'I'm Spartacus'?" asks Liam.

"In Roman times?" I prompt. He looks at me blankly. "It's where everyone stands up and says they're Spartacus, to protect the *real* Spartacus from getting in trouble. Cos the Romans can't punish all of them. Except, *actually* they do all get crucif—"

"Cool," interrupts Gemma. Then she stands up on her chair. "I'm Spartacus!" she shouts.

Liam laughs delightedly, and stands up on his chair too. "No, *I'm Spartacus!*" he yells.

Mark and someone called Rob climb up on to their chairs. "I'm Spartacus!"

People start giggling and standing up on their chairs. I'm sure they're doing it more for the fun and novelty of joining in than because they really care about who drew on Olivia's bag.

Suddenly nearly everyone is on their chairs chanting "I'm Spartacus!"

Jas pushes her chair out and pulls me to my feet. "*When in Rome*," she quips, and we join everyone on the chairs. "I'm Spartacus!"

Olivia looks like she's about to cry and then runs out of the room. *Good*, I try to think. I don't need to feel guilty about this. She started it. She had it coming. It's payback.

"What on earth is going on in here?" Mrs Wiggins enters the room holding her cup of tea.

"I'm Spartacus!" the class tell her as one, looking amused and pleased with themselves.

"*None of you are Spartacus!* Sit down immediately!" Mrs Wiggins looks like she is trying not to laugh.

Everyone sits down happily and gets on with the lesson. This would have easily been class detention with most other teachers. Definitely in maths. The art teachers are so laid-back, they don't even notice when a student is missing.

Oh my god, I just *won*, I realise. I just vanquished and publically humiliated Olivia. *Ha*. I just totally got brilliant revenge. She must be ruing and lamenting the day she crossed me *now*.

I *am* like the Count of Monte Cristo after all. (I'm assuming. I still have no idea how that story ends.) But I got my revenge. This is exactly what I wanted. It's weird; I don't feel *quite* as euphoric as I anticipated. But who cares? The point is: I am *brilliant* at revenge.*

* *May not be brilliant at revenge.*

CHAPTER TWENTY–SEVEN

They say *be careful what you wish for*. And to be honest, I generally always have been. For instance, I never wished I was a princess. Partly because when we learnt about the French and Russian Revolutions, and beheadings and stuff, it didn't sound like things tended to end very well for them.

Why do I feel *guilty* about Olivia? *Because you got everyone to stand on their chairs to agree how much they hated her?* says a voice in my head that sounds a lot like Jas. (Which is weird, because we are friends now and Jas totally stood on her chair too.)

I defend myself to my imaginary Jas voice. *Inadvertently*. I *inadvertently* got everyone to stand on their chairs to agree how much they hated her. I didn't *mean* for that to happen. It was mainly Gemma.

Fine, you're completely innocent then, says the voice, sarcastically.

So, what then? Should I find her and apologise? Confess I *did* write on her bag? No – she'd probably record it on her phone and I'd have detention for a term. Or be expelled.

And *so what* if Olivia now scurries past me and won't even make eye contact? Big deal. I mean, she still does it in an snarky way, like she's making a point she has to get away from me as quickly as possible, like I'm *evil* and *toxic*, not like she's scared of me or anything. But, hey – it's definitely *easier* than her making comments about me all the time.

And *anyway*, Olivia repeatedly humiliated *me* in front of everyone. I've just given her a taste of her own medicine. So *ha*. I insist on *ha*. This is a *ha* situation and that's the end of it. I don't feel guilty. Shut up.

And actually, I should be *super-happy* – I've got literally everything I wanted:

(a) My best friend is my best friend again.

(b) My parents are *getting on* – they've both said they now realise that they need to rise above their petty squabbles and be there for me. Whatever.

(c) I vanquished Olivia.

It's so weird, but I still have this sort of restless, bored feeling sometimes. And I keep wondering what BUTTS are up to, even though I don't *really* want to hang around with them. I don't think.

In other news, it turns out that when your dad is "very lenient and understanding" (his words) about you disappearing off to a launderette in the "middle of the night" (again, his words – it was more like 6 p.m.) you end up:

(a) Not being pedantic enough to quibble about the fact it was actually 6 p.m. when you left.

(b) Agreeing to do "something fun" (his words) like *going to a farm*.

My words to describe this situation would be quite different. For example, they might include:

(a) "Not fun."

(b) "Really not a *great* use of a Saturday."

(c) "Not a farm."

"Dad, I think this is more of a petting zoo than a farm," I tell him, as we walk past some chickens.

"No, it is a farm," says Dad. "They sell eggs and milk and jam and stuff. I'm pretty sure that makes it a farm."

I think that makes it a *gift shop*, I think secretly, but hold my tongue. I must try to look on the bright side: at least Jas is here; it's only a *bit* boring; I … couldn't even get to three reasons.

I *think* Jas and I might be far too old for this type of thing now. But it's fine, it's fine. I'm fine.

"Shall we buy the food so we can feed the donkey?" Dad offers jovially.

Plus look how happy my dad is. I did that. Just by agreeing to come here. It's like I have magic powers. Really rubbish ones, but still.

"Sure," I say enthusiastically. Then, more quietly to Jas, "is this OK for you? You're not … bored or anything, are you?"

"No, this is great." Jas is smiling at the cute animals. "I haven't done anything like this in *ages*."

Yes, because it's age appropriate for five-year-olds, a nasty voice in my head wants to say sneeringly. *Be nice, be nice.* Some toddlers run past us. So there are toddlers here. *Big deal.* I don't care. I'm having *fun*. I'm not embarrassed.

Dad gets the food and we go over to the donkeys. "Remember, you have to hold your hand completely flat," advises Dad.

Jas giggles. "It tickles!"

It does tickle. It's fun. I said it was fun. I mean, not as much fun as learning to jump off the high diving board. That was *amazing*. But … gentle fun can be fun too.

We queue up with the tiny children and feed some baby lambs some milk. It's very cute. Jas and I are *much* braver than the wailing three-year-old who's scared of lambs for some reason. What a loser that kid is.

Then, after we've fed some goats too, we wash our hands *thoroughly*, as per the sign, and go to the café. We all get cream teas and sit outside in the sun watching the animals. It's nice. *Definitely.*

"Pssst, Ella, over here!" Mark summons me under the main hall staircase at the end of Wednesday lunch.

Oh thank god, finally something exciting. I mean, oh no, what does he want?

I wonder if he's going to confess his undying love for me? He might— Oh, OK, all of BUTTS are here too.

"Um, hi?" I try to act natural. "What's up?"

"We've got a brilliant idea for a prank!" Liam grins.

"Oh yeah?" I say. My excitement about Mark is crashing into trepidation about this. But, still, sort of *excited trepidation*.

Gemma looks around, then leans in towards me. "We're going to *egg* Mr Brown's house!" she whispers, elated. "We just found out where he lives."

"WHAT? *Why?*" I ask.

"Because he keeps giving us detention for no reason," says Mark.

"I thought he keeps giving you detention because you keep doing really dangerous things in his lessons that he could get in loads of trouble for?" I say.

Mark shrugs, amused. "Potato, pot*ar*to."

"So," Gemma grins, "you in?"

"Um… I'll think about it," I say evasively.

I finally remember to look at Mark's feet and they are pointing at me! OMG, that means he must fancy me! Maybe I *should* do this? Maybe our eyes will meet across a crowded— OK, what actually is *wrong* with me?

"Well, don't think about it too long or we won't let you become one of us," says Liam.

Wait, *what*?

Oh god, am I in BUTTS* now?

May not actually be in BUTTS.

CHAPTER TWENTY-EIGHT

I'd be lying if I said I wasn't conflicted. I *am*. But I'm also giggling along with the others in nervous anticipation and excitement, as we walk towards Mr Brown's house. We're going to *egg* a teacher's house! At night! That's *so bad*!

The trick is, I realise, not to *over-think* it. Don't over-think the fact that I've just *snuck out* for the first (or technically second) time in my life and no one knows where I am. Don't over-think the fact that I've just convinced my dad I'm trustworthy and now that's almost certainly over. And *definitely* don't over-think the fact I am about to do something *illegal*.

I wonder if my dad will have noticed I'm gone yet. Maybe he won't even notice *at all*? And really that's a problem for tomorrow. *Don't think about it*.

Gemma and Liam have brought a box of twelve eggs each. Mark has brought some balaclavas, and thinks we should film some of the egging to put on YouTube.

I privately think that's a terrible idea, as it'll be proof that we did it. If I've learnt anything from the detective shows on the Disney Channel, it's that a simple thing like a recognisable watch strap could give us away. Plus I think their plan to become prankster YouTube stars is also flawed because most of the people I've seen that do these kinds of pranks are doing it to people that they know, who will eventually find it funny, or do it back to them, so it's sort of almost fair. What we're about to do is technically criminal damage and we could be prosecuted for it. *I think*. The Disney Channel isn't very specific about the legal technicalities.

"This is going to be so fun!" Gemma giggles gleefully as we walk down a leafy residential street.

"Yeah!" I giggle back.

I'm still conflicted, though. So I just keep trying not to think about it.

Don't picture how sad Mr Brown's face will look

when he sees the smashed eggs all over his house. I gulp. That's really unfair, isn't it?

Damn, I accidentally just thought about it.

No, I shake my head.

What if we get caught and arrested, and my dad is ashamed and I get sent to prison?

Well, I won't get send to *prison*. On the Disney Channel, only *adults* get sent to prison. Bad kids tend to end up just having to clean toilets and pick up litter and stuff. Or, at the very least, gunged in green slime. Or maybe that's *CBeebies*? *Hmmm.* Maybe kids' TV isn't the most reliable source for how criminal law works?

Stop thinking! I order myself.

I'm starting to feel kind of stressed and panicked, like this isn't actually a good idea at all.

"You all right, Ella?" Mark asks. "You've gone quiet."

"You're not chickening out, are you?" says Gemma accusingly.

I can't tell them I'm having second thoughts because I *like* teachers now. That since Miss Gaskew gave me back my bracelets I've realised teachers are human people with more than two dimensions;

that they have nice sides, and thoughts and feelings too; that if we prick them they will bleed; if we egg their houses, they will feel really sad about that... I mean, I especially can't phrase it like that, with half a butchered Shakespeare quote in the middle... I can't say any of that and also I'm not supposed to tell anyone Miss Gaskew broke her precious protocol to give me my bracelets back.

"No, of course not," I reply unconvincingly.

They appear satisfied.

I wonder if I can somehow tip off Mr Brown that we're coming, and he can scare us away before we get there? But I have no way of contacting him. Plus snitching is too heinous a crime. They'd know it was me.

"We're nearly there!" Liam calls out excitedly.

"Awesome!" says Mark.

"These eggs have gone off," says Gemma. "They're gonna stink! This is gonna be brilliant!" Everyone giggles excitedly.

"Right, this is the place," says Liam, and we stop outside a semi-detached house with a car parked on the driveway and a swing set, slide and Wendy house on the front lawn.

I suddenly go cold. He has kids! Oh my god, *he has kids*. We can't do this. We can't do this to *kids*. It's too horrible. The kids are completely innocent. They don't deserve to wake up to an egging.

Mark puts on a balaclava. Gemma starts handing out the eggs.

"Stop! Stop!" I hiss at them, running over.

"Start with the windows, I reckon," Gemma tells Liam.

"No, no, you guys! Look! There's a slide!" I whisper-shout.

"Oh yes! Good idea," says Gemma approvingly. "Let's get the slide!"

"NO!" I shout a bit louder than I'd intended.

They all stop what they're doing and stare at me.

"Keep your voice down," says Liam crossly.

"What's your problem?" asks Gemma.

Am I really about to tell them all they *can't* do this? The three scariest, baddest people in my year?

I think I might be… I'm about to tell them they can't do this. Or am I…?

Yes. I am.

My certainty gives me courage. *I want to stop them.* More than I care if they like me, or what happens to me after that. More than I care even if Mark likes me. He suddenly doesn't look so great to me with my newfound confidence.

What would my dad do? Maybe I can talk them round using cold hard logic...

"We have to abort this mission," I tell them. "He has kids."

"*So?*" Liam smirks.

"So the kids haven't done anything wrong," I say. "They don't deserve for their slide to get ruined."

"They're probably horrible little spoilt brats," says Gemma. "Look at all this stuff. They've practically got their own *park* in their front garden."

"*Yeah*," says Liam. "They need to see how the other half live for a change."

"Yeah," agrees Gemma.

"How does egging a slide show them how the other half live?" I ask.

They all glare at me crossly. "Stop being such a snob," says Gemma.

OK, logic isn't working.

What would Mum do? She'd get results whatever it took ... shouting, threatening, screaming... *Hey*...

"OK, look. If you throw eggs at any of this stuff,

234

I'll *scream*," I say. "Really loudly. All the lights will come on. Everyone will come running, and you'll be caught."

I mean, I'd probably be caught too. I guess it's mutually assured destruction, like the nuclear threat?

"You wouldn't *dare*!" Gemma is incensed.

I hold my ground. "I *would*."

"We'll just throw eggs at *you*," says Gemma.

I grin. "Maybe that's not such a bad idea."

"What?" says Gemma crossly.

"OK," I say calmly. "You have a load of eggs that you want to throw at something. I am something. How about we make a deal? If you promise not to throw eggs at this house, car or any of this kids' stuff, you can throw them all at me. I will stand still on the pavement for ten seconds, then I'm going to run."

"OK," says Mark. "But I want to film it on my phone too, for YouTube."

"OK," I say, "but then I will only stand still for three seconds."

"Five," says Gemma.

"Deal."

Everyone shakes my hand, and gets into position. I feel very briefly like I'm on *The Apprentice*. And

I've just made the worst and *stupidest* deal that anyone has ever made on *The Apprentice*. Like, I would *definitely* be fired first.

And then they start throwing the eggs.

CHAPTER TWENTY-NINE

"What in the— When did you— Where in the *hell* have you been?" Dad's astonishment turns to anger and then to confusion, as he takes in my appearance at the front door. "Is that *egg*?"

There's nothing else for it. I'm going to have to tell him what's happened. I accept that this could be a terrible idea.

"Yes," I say, squinting through the egg. "I can explain everything. But first I think I should take a shower."

"Um… Yes, OK, I suppose you *had* better have a shower," Dad says, bamboozled. I turn to go upstairs. "And, Ella?" I turn back, still squinting through one eye. "You should use cold water to wash the eggs out of your hair. Hot water might cook them."

"Excellent tip, thanks," I tell him, and go upstairs.

If I had to rate being covered in rotten eggs vs. having a cold shower, I think it would be a tie. My teeth are chattering. This is so grim.

As soon as I'm convinced I've got rid of enough of the eggs, i.e. two shampoos, I turn the hot water back on and try to recover.

I got *gunged*. A punishment worthy of kids' TV. *Kids' TV karma*. Does this absolve me of my crimes? Even though being pelted with eggs was absolutely disgusting, and this was definitely the worst shower of my life, I still feel oddly pleased with myself, and *somehow* empowered.

You can't always solve a problem with logic and you can't always solve a problem by yelling. But sometimes you *can* solve a problem by thinking outside the box and getting covered in eggs.

I come down to the living room and tell Dad all about how I've become friends with a group of people at school who are sometimes badly behaved and rude to the teachers. I tell him that I watched them do graffiti, and even shoplifted with them, but that I felt very guilty, so I put back the hairbrush that I stole.

I also tell him that I sneaked out with the explicit intention of going with them to egg a teacher's house. But that when I got there I couldn't go through with it, and so convinced them to egg me instead.

My dad sits listening to the whole story in total silence. Then when I've finished he finally says, "Right. OK then."

"And, Dad, listen, I want you to know that I really appreciate the open dialogue you started after the launderette incident, and I'm very sorry I sneaked out without telling you." (Mum's therapy speak is rubbing off on me.)

"Right," says Dad warily. "Noted."

"I have now told you everything in an attempt to be completely honest," I say. "How you respond to this information may influence how truthful I feel I am able to be with you in the future. But for what it's worth I feel like I have already learnt my lesson and been punished by being, you know, covered in eggs."

Dad scratches the back of his head. "I don't quite know what to say."

"Well." I pause. "If I may be so bold as to make a suggestion…?"

Dad sighs. "Go on."

"Uh, how about… You are disappointed and yet proud of me for telling you the truth?" I offer optimistically. "You are impressed that I sacrificed myself with an egging, and agree I need no further punishment?"

"Um. *Well*." Dad pauses. "I *am* proud of you for telling me the truth. But…" He sits up straighter in his chair. "I am also very angry and incredibly disappointed in your behaviour. That's not how I … *we* brought you up. *Graffiti? Stealing?* You know better than that." He takes a deep breath before continuing.

"That's right, I do. If you remember the bit in the story where I didn't actually *do* those things? I merely observed the graffiti, and I *undid* the shoplifting."

"You deliberately snuck out again, when I explicitly told you not to, practically *seconds* after the launderette kerfuffle."

Seconds, that is *such* an exaggeration. Dad is really paraphrasing the hell out of what happened.

Dad continues. "I'm delighted you have decided to

240

be honest with me. But I can't let you go unpunished."

"Oh," I say, my spirits sinking.

"I can't believe I'm saying this," sighs Dad, "but I think I need your mother's advice."

Well, this should be relatively painless, I think, as Mum's taxi pulls up outside. Oh *sure*, she's too busy to be on time to meet me for *fun times*, but she's free as a bird to pop round and help *punish* me at the drop of a hat. Anyway. I mustn't panic. Mum's the *fun one,* remember.

Dad lets Mum in and they sit down on the sofa, opposite me.

"Mum, I—"

"*What ON EARTH were you thinking!?*"

This is a rhetorical question it turns out. If I try to answer it, she cuts me off with:

"Well, you weren't thinking *at all*, were you?"

And if I try to answer *that*… Well, you get the picture.

Mum's yelling and screaming goes on for quite some time. She's got stamina, I'll give her that. And I can't even get a word in edgeways to defend myself. By the time she finally says, "*Well?* Do you have anything to say for yourself?" all my sassy rejoinders seem redundant. I feel deflated and defeated.

So much for Mum being the *fun* one.

Finally Dad takes over. "We need to select a suitable punishment," he says.

"Have you got something in mind?" Mum asks.

"Yes, and I'm not sure Ella will like it," he says.

"She's not supposed to like it," replies Mum.

"Yes," says Dad. He clears his throat. "Ella, we appreciate that you've come clean, but in light of your behaviour I'm afraid I'm taking away your mobile phone privileges for a week."

"A week?" scoffs Mum. "That's nowhere near long enough. You're losing that mobile phone for a *year, young lady!*"

"That's an awfully long time," says Dad. "How about a month?"

Enough is enough, I decide. "Can I say something here? You were both annoyed with me for *not* having my phone with me at the launderette. Isn't it actually going to be very annoying for you to not be able to track me down?"

"Well, you won't be going anywhere because you'll be grounded for a year," says Mum.

"Or a month?" says Dad.

"I know!" says Mum. She jumps up and starts rummaging through a drawer. "Ha! Perfect!" She comes back and hands me a huge grey piece of plastic. "*This* can be your phone."

"You can't be serious!" I howl. "I can't carry that thing around! It's like a brick! This phone looks older than I am!"

"Well, almost," Dad laughs. "It might be ten years old… They wouldn't let us trade it in. I don't think it's even Internet-compatible."

"So it can pretty much only be used as a phone or for texting," says Mum.

"Yes," agrees Dad. "So no more chat-snapping or whats-booking."

Mum and I are temporarily united in the briefest disdainful look at Dad's ignorance.

"Mum, come on!" I implore, turning to her. "I thought you wanted to treat me like a grown-up. You let me get the bus at night by myself. Why are you punishing me so dreadfully like this?"

"That was when I *trusted* you," she replies. "Also, your dad has since put me straight on your proper curfew."

"And it certainly isn't ten o'clock!" scoffs Dad.

"But I never said it was!" *Technically*.

"You need to earn my trust back," says Mum. Who does she think she is? *The Godfather?* She should be earning *my* trust. Or something.

"So I have to use this *thing* for a whole month? *This is so unfair!!!*"

"That's your dad's punishment," says Mum. (*What?* She seemed pretty involved in that punishment to me.) "*I* still have to punish you."

"*What?*"

"So, let's see." She settles back down on the sofa. "My punishment is that you can help me do up my flat."

"What?" This seems *very* like a *kids' TV* karma kind of punishment. In a slightly unsettling cleaning-toilets sort of way.

"You heard. There's loads to do. You can help me at weekends while you're grounded."

"That's slave labour," I reply. Though actually I kind of like this idea: spending more time at Mum's house, getting to know each other better ... a montage scene where we wear white overalls and then high-five...?

"We'll start by retiling my bathroom. You're never too young to learn a trade. You don't know what you'll be good at until you try. I don't want you to repeat my mistakes or ever feel helpless, like you can't do things. Hell, I didn't know how to rewire a plug until I was *thirty*." She scoffs like this is ridiculous. "But I mean it, Ella. No one should ever be able to make you think you have to do things you don't want to do. Believe in yourself. You are smart and usually right."

"Fine." I sigh dramatically, so that they think this is a proper punishment and don't *up* it any more. Maybe the library's got some great books on plastering. And I'll learn to be GREAT at plastering...*

* *May not actually be great at plastering.*

CHAPTER THIRTY

I'm not sure my dad fully grasps the concept of being *grounded* because he still lets me go swimming on Sunday. I think he just *really* likes to have Sundays to himself, though he insists he's only making exceptions for things that are "exercise" or "educational". I'm glad he has laid out these excellent loopholes ready for exploitation.

It's handy too, because I have one more person to confess to and that's Jas. I tell her *everything*. It feels good to get it all off my chest.

"I knew you weren't telling me everything!" She's amazed.

After she finally stops telling me she can't *believe* it but simultaneously *knew* it on some level, she says she thinks my hair looks really shiny and glossy today.

I laugh.

"Eggs are meant to be really good for your hair. Look." She googles it on her phone and shows me as we walk to swimming.

I take her phone and read it as we walk along.

Jas takes my arm and guides me away from a postbox.

"Damn it," I say, looking up. "I could have just used *lukewarm* water. I didn't need to freeze my nips off in the shower after all."

"Ha!" Jas takes her phone back and puts it in her pocket. "I just hope you haven't caught salmonella from all those eggs."

"That's not possible, is it?"

"I don't know," Jas teases.

"Google it!" I tell her. "I don't have a phone!"

"Mate, your brick is the equivalent of *ten phones*."

"In weight alone," I agree.

And all the emojis come out as question marks. I have no idea what anyone my age is saying. Is this what it's like to be *Dad?* No wonder he's so confused and grumpy.

"Ninety-seven views!" Gemma tells me proudly at registration on Monday morning, shoving her phone in my face as I enter the form room.

This will sound weird, but I'd sort of almost forgotten all about BUTTS. I feel like the me who wanted to hang out with them was a me of a hundred years ago.

I feel no pangs, or pull towards them at all now. Not even Mark. I look right into his eyes and nothing happens.

"This is my favourite bit," says Liam. "Ha ha! How good is that?" The rest of BUTTS chuckle.

I wonder briefly if all ninety-seven views is just them admiring their handiwork.

"You know what, Ella?" says Gemma. "You're calm, you are. *Mad*. But calm."

"Thanks," I tell her, and head over to my desk.

At first break time, I do a possibly stupid thing. I go up to Olivia in the canteen. She's waiting for Sasha and Grace to come back from the can machine, so I have her on her own for a moment.

"What do *you* want?" she asks me, leaning against the window tiredly.

"I just wanted to say I'm sorry about what happened with your bag and the *I'm Spartacus* thing."

"*Great.* We done now?"

"And if it's any consolation, this happened to me." I hold up the video, which I have primed on Jas's phone.

Olivia watches me get egged and a happy smirk spreads across her face. "Good," she says. Then the smirk is replaced by a look of bafflement. "Why on *earth* would you show me that? I would never have shown *you.*"

"I don't know. It's just, I guess, a kind of peace offering. You don't need to be nasty to me any more. Can't we just leave it?"

"I wasn't *nasty* to you," says Olivia haughtily. "I was only ever *joking*. It's not *my* fault if you can't take a joke. I could have said even worse things…" She stops herself. "OK, fine. I was a *bit* nasty."

"Thank you," I say.

"What's *with* you?" Olivia looks confused.

Sasha and Grace return with three cans of Diet Coke. "What's going on?" asks Grace.

"Nothing," says Olivia.

"Causing a bit of congestion here, girls," says Mr

Brown, who is patrolling the canteen again. "Move away from the can machine once you've got your drinks, so other people can get to it."

"Oh, we were just leaving, sir," says Olivia loftily. "It smells of *egg* round here anyway." Then she quickly looks back at me. "That was a *joke*," she emphasises.

"Good one," I say.

They walk off. I hear Sasha ask her if she's friends with me now, and Olivia say no before they are out of earshot.

I guess only time will tell if that was a good idea, but it feels liberating to ride my mad little burst of confidence for a bit longer.

I notice Mr Brown is wearing a *SpongeBob SquarePants* tie. "Did your kids buy you that tie?" I ask him.

"What?" says Mr Brown, looking confused. "I don't have any kids."

"*What?* I mean... Oh, really?" I say, and back awkwardly away.

What? I start heading out of the canteen as quickly as possible. *Oh my god, it wasn't his house! It wasn't even his house!* Those *idiots*! I stopped them from egging a complete and utter random stranger's house on Saturday night! Also, I have just inadvertently insulted Mr Brown's tie. *Whoops.*

"It wasn't his house!" I blurt to Gemma, as soon as I make it back to the form room before the end of break.

"What?" Gemma looks confused. The rest of BUTTS gather round.

"Mr Brown doesn't even have kids! I was just talking to him. It can't have been his house on Saturday! Where did you get that address from?"

"The Internet," says Liam.

"There's probably a million Mr Browns," I tell him. "You just picked a random one. It wasn't him."

"Wow. Good job you stopped us egging that house then," says Gemma, and they all laugh.

Oh god, they are *idiots.* Jas was right all along. *Ughh,* BUTTS.

Another upshot of everything that's happened is Dad and I now sometimes talk to each other like hippies that have gone on a psychology course together. We seem to preface everything we know the other one doesn't want to hear with the sentence, "In the interests of maintaining an open dialogue…"

So breakfast can go like this:

"Dad, in the interests of maintaining an open dialogue, your T-shirt looks kind of weird tucked into your trousers like that."

"Well, in the interests of maintaining an open dialogue, I'm not sure it's your place to say."

It's refreshing and kind of funny.

I text Jas that I can't believe how well everything has worked out, and I get back,

> ???

> MATE, YOU KNOW I CAN'T READ EMOJIS ON THIS PHONE!

> Punked. I literally wrote ??? that time + U fell for it.

> Idiot.

> Sorry ????

and

?????

come back.

Aaarrgh. I throw my anachronistic piece of junk on the table.

Breathe. *It's fine, it's fine.* It's only for a bit longer. And it has made me appreciate how lucky I really am.

And I genuinely do think things have worked out really well. (Apart from when I accidentally got paint on Mum's fridge.) Plus my parents are getting on much better and Dad sometimes gives me a *lift* to my slave labour at Mum's flat now. We're all such grown-ups.

Overall I feel much better. I actually think I might definitely be OK now.*

* I really could be OK. I've got a good feeling about this one.

ACKNOWLEDGEMENTS

Massive thanks to Kirsty Stansfield, Suzy Jenvey, Lindsey Fraser, Kathryn Ross, Kate Wilson, Catherine Stokes, Fiona Scoble, Nicola Theobald, Tom Bonnick, Rebecca Mason and everyone at Nosy Crow, who have been so fantastic. And also thank YOU for reading.